Suddenly Elizabeth heard the whickering cry of an owl. She froze. Then she whistled and called softly to her brothers, "Big? Little?"

"What?" Big said, his face pale even under the grime.

Elizabeth tipped her head in slow motion in the direction of the blockhouse. Big knew what to do. He held tight to his brother and the two took off in a gallop toward the open gate. Elizabeth gulped. She scanned the trees and listened hard.

No movement. No sound.

Nothing.

Yet she knew. Somewhere deep in the darkening woods someone was watching them.

Books by Laurie Lawlor

The Worm Club
How to Survive Third Grade
Addie Across the Prairie
Addie's Long Summer
Addie's Dakota Winter
George on His Own
Gold in the Hills
Little Women *(movie tie-in)*

Heartland series
Heartland: Come Away with Me
Heartland: Take to the Sky
Heartland: Luck Follows Me

American Sisters series
West Along the Wagon Road 1852
A *Titanic* Journey Across the Sea 1912
Voyage to a Free Land 1630
Adventure on the Wilderness Road 1775
Crossing the Colorado Rockies 1864
Down the Río Grande 1829
Horseback on the Boston Post Road 1704
Exploring the Chicago World's Fair 1893
Pacific Odyssey to California 1905

American Sisters
Adventure on the Wilderness Road
1775

Laurie Lawlor

Published by POCKET BOOKS
New York London Toronto Sydney Singapore

This book is a work of fiction. Names, characters, places and incidents are products of the author's imagination or are used fictitiously. Any resemblance to actual events or locales or persons, living or dead, is entirely coincidental.

A Minstrel Book published by
POCKET BOOKS, a division of Simon & Schuster, Inc.
1230 Avenue of the Americas, New York, NY 10020

Originally published in hardcover in 1999 by Pocket Books

ISBN: 0-671-77568-5

First Minstrel Books paperback printing May 2001

10 9 8 7 6 5 4 3 2 1

Cover illustration by Dennis Lyall

Printed in the U.S.A.

For Adam

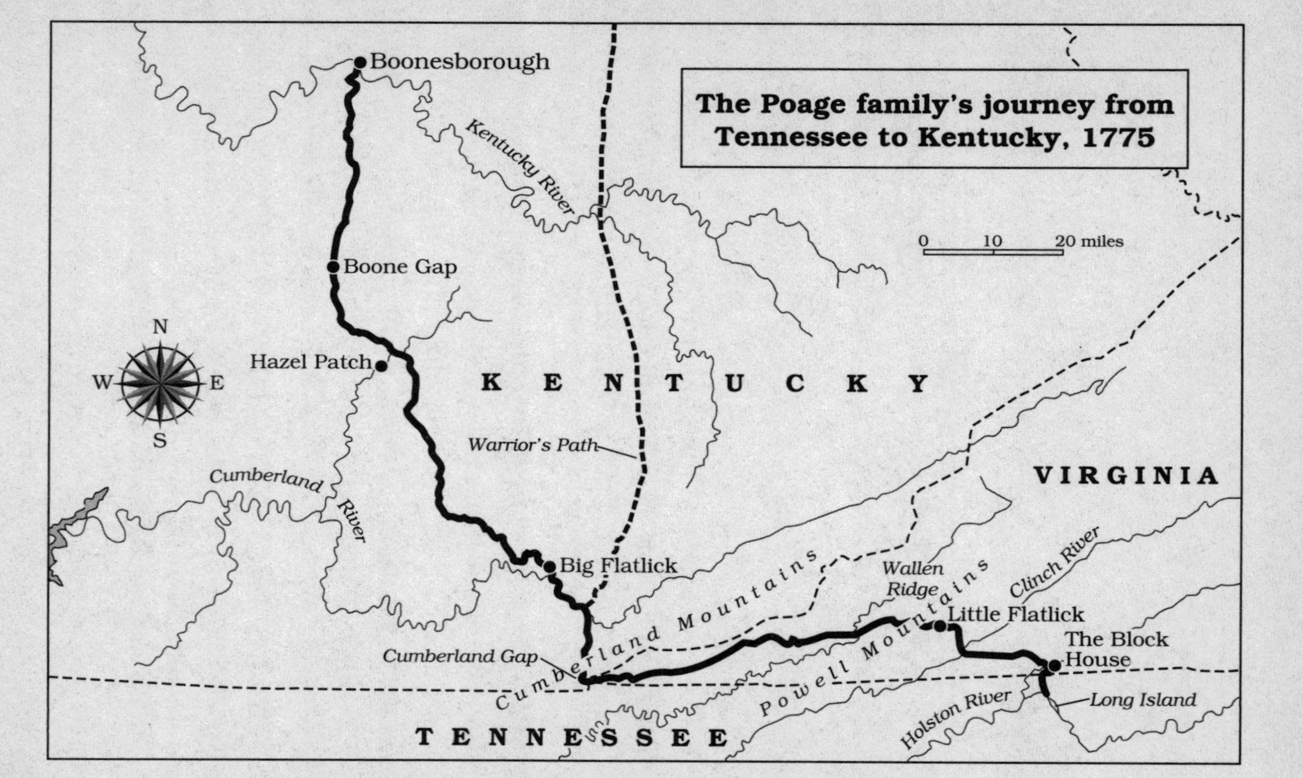
The Poage family's journey from Tennessee to Kentucky, 1775
Boonesborough
Kentucky River
Boone Gap
Hazel Patch
N
W
E
S
KENTUCKY
Warrior's Path
Cumberland River
Big Flatlick
0 10 20 miles
VIRGINIA
Cumberland Mountains
Wallen Ridge
Powell Mountains
Clinch River
Little Flatlick
The Block House
Long Island
Holston River
Cumberland Gap
TENNESSEE

The woods seemed to shine this September morning. Elizabeth Poage walked along swinging an empty wooden bucket, listening for her younger brothers. Nicknamed Big and Little, five-year-old Robert and three-year-old Joseph had dashed ahead on the trail to the spring as soon as they were out of sight of the Holston settlement. Elizabeth, who was eleven, didn't worry about her brothers' rough and tumble. Big and Little knew enough not to bite into a buckeye, chew poison ivy, or eat a bright poison oak berry. Most important, they had been drilled to be vigilant because behind any tree or any bush, an Indian with a scalping knife might be watching, waiting.

Elizabeth dropped the bucket. She took a seat on a stump within earshot of her brothers, who shouted and laughed and whacked each other with broken branches. She closed her eyes and enjoyed her hard-earned, rare moment of privacy. The familiar musky scent of rotting leaves and damp wood filled the air. All around her came the constant, quieter-than-rain sound of more leaves falling. *Tat-a-tat-tat-a-tat* called a woodpecker from somewhere deep in the woods. Maybe clear to the river. She tried to imagine how far that woodpecker could see once it left the Holston and soared high above the forest and the hills. *Maybe all the way to Caintuck.*

She opened her pale blue eyes and scanned the quilt-size scraps of sky she could see between towering trees overhead. Mountains and trees had surrounded her all her life. To the east loomed the Blue Ridge. To the west stood the gaunt hills of the Cumberlands. If she looked north, she saw the rugged ridges of the Clinch Mountains; south tumbled away the peaks of Chimney Top and the Bays Mountain Range.

Just as she could name each mountain around the settlement, she also knew the subtle autumn color of each type of tree and plant. She could pick out shoemake—red, very red, but different from dogwood red. She scanned another distant grove and could tell cedar green from pine green. Beyond were the clear yellow of hickory and chestnut, buck and poplar, red and gold of maple and sweet gum, bloodred of black gum, and the faded bronze of oaks. Soon all the leaves would fall. The only green remaining would be found in the cane brakes along the river and creek bottoms and in thin, sandy places where laurel and ivy managed to flourish.

By then Elizabeth and her family would be far, far away from these familiar woods. She sighed. She didn't want to think about leaving. Not now.

From her belt she pulled a letter, the first ever to come for her alone. She had read it so many times, she knew every word by heart. Even so, she carefully unfolded the dirty, smudged sheet of paper. With her finger she followed each line and read aloud, if only for the lovely sound the words made.

July 30, 1775

Dear Elizabeth;

I would much rather visit then writ to you, but when I think of the distance between us, I be quite disparin to ever see you again. I dont hanker after the Holston no more. The danger is too turrable. In Pennsylvania we aren't afeard of Indians. Crost the Conostogo, a good deal uneasie should my sickness return. The Conostogo is a creek with fine prospects around it. After refreshing ourselves we tooke a walk up the Creek. I never saw such a beautiful civilized place. You cant imagine how I long'd for you to join our little Party. Me and my cousins sit under shade trees and eat ham and biscuit. Papa promises to buy me a red cloak to wear when school starts. The school is a pretty stone Building with real desks for each of us. I must hurry up and finish this. Mr. Arnold is going west and promises to tote our letters. I hope this reaches you before you and your family head into those dark mountains of Caintuck. Tell Martha I wisht her well and not to disremember me.

Your ever affectionate friend,
Parthena Spikner
Lancaster, Pennsylvania

Slowly Elizabeth folded the letter. *A pretty stone building with real desks for each of us.* She could just imagine frail, ten-year-old Parthena walking to school in her bright red cloak—maybe with her precious storybook under an arm. Parthena who knew how to read, too. Parthena who could make ghosts disappear by crossing her left thumb over her index finger, drawing a long breath, and chanting, "Skip-i-to! Skip-i-to!"

Elizabeth sighed, thinking of her best friend. In the Holston settlement, school was taught by Mr. Feeny in the back of his noisy, dimly lit store. Elizabeth, her nine-year-old sister, Martha, Parthena, and four other students shared one copy of Dilworth's *Grammar* and read in loud voices from tattered four-year-old newspapers. They sat with their feet dangling from backless seats made of split halves of logs. Mr. Feeny demonstrated how to form the alphabet on a smooth board using the end of a charred stick. Eventually Elizabeth learned to write on precious sheets of paper with a pen cut from a goose quill and ink made from pokeberries.

It was a sacrifice for her parents to send her and Martha to school. "You can go if you do chores before and after," said Pa, who could write and read some from the Bible, the only book the family owned. Ma couldn't read a word of Scripture and could only make a mark to signify her name. Pa paid for their lessons with bowls and spoons and trenchers carved from tiger-striped maple wood and a table and a set of chairs made from oak. When Mr. Feeny protested that Pa had given far more than his fair share, Pa said, "I don't like to owe no man nothing."

After the last attack in late spring, the Spikners and three other families moved east. Corn planting and harvest kept the remaining students too busy to attend lessons. When Mr. Feeny officially canceled school because there weren't enough students, Martha whooped with glee. "Good riddance!" she shouted.

"No harm done," proclaimed ancient Aunt Genevy, the only midwife for miles. "Everybody knows book learning's a waste of time."

Mr. Feeny went back to waiting on customers in the store. Elizabeth went back to spinning, cooking, cleaning, and taking care of her four younger brothers and sisters. Unlike Martha, Elizabeth had enjoyed school. She missed shaping mysterious scratch marks into words. She missed reading from Parthena's storybook about places far beyond their mountains—places with palaces and princesses and talking cats who wore big boots. Now there was no more school, no more Parthena, no more stories, and no more make-believe. Worse yet, tomorrow they were leaving for Kentucky, and on that long, lonesome journey Elizabeth knew the only companion near her age would be Martha.

Tell Martha I wisht her well and not to disremember me. Elizabeth frowned. This was the only part that marred Parthena's otherwise perfect letter. *Why, oh why, did she have to mention that pest?* Elizabeth had never liked sharing Parthena with her sister. The three girls could scarcely play blindman's bluff or hide-and-seek without Martha's changing the rules and introducing invisible poison arrows or hungry panthers. Someone would start crying, and the games would end in angry words.

Even when there were fights and misunderstandings, Parthena never blamed Martha. She never stopped playing with her. She said she admired her spunk and imagination. "Nothing's ever dull around your sister," she told Elizabeth. "There's nobody else quite like her."

To Elizabeth, Martha was nothing but a bellyache. If she could have, she would trade her for a helpful, ladylike older sister. *Someone wise and thoughtful and pretty. Someone I can talk to. Someone not one bit like Martha.*

"Elizabeth!" Big shouted.

Elizabeth jumped to her feet.

"Elizabeth!" His voice was louder, shriller now.

Indians! She jammed the letter into her belt, grabbed the bucket, and sprinted toward the place she had heard her brother calling. She found Little unhurt and crouching on the ground. No Cherokee or Shawnee in sight. She examined Little's dirty face and ripped shirt. "Where's Big?" she demanded, her heart still galloping in her chest. "Why'd he scream like that?"

Little pointed to the top of a slender fir tree that shook mysteriously. There was Big, swinging back and forth, holding on for dear life to the highest branch. As the wind blew, the slender tree bucked and shifted back and forth.

"Help!" screamed Big.

Elizabeth grinned. "What's wrong?" she asked sweetly.

"Can't get down. Shirt's hooked."

Elizabeth placed her hands on her hips. "Serves you right. Remember last time? I warned you not to climb tall fir trees and ride them like some wild horse."

"I ain't riding no wild horse," Big growled. "I'm stuck."

"Fine. We'll just go to Caintuck without you. Won't we, Little?"

Little's blue eyes bulged with terror. If Big were left behind, he would be on his own for the first time in his life. Ferociously he yanked on Elizabeth's skirt. "Get him," Little begged.

"Why should I? Good riddance. Let the turkey buzzards eat him." Elizabeth looked up at her dangling brother. "Bide where you be."

Big let out a horrible string of Pa's oaths. In spite of Ma's protests, Pa was one of the most famous cussers this side of the Holston. Little began to whimper like a pup pulled from the warm comfort of its litter.

Elizabeth couldn't stand to see Little cry. "All right," she said gruffly. "I'll rescue him. But this is the last time, Big, you hear?" She hiked up her homespun shift and petticoat and tied them around her waist to free up her strong, long legs and bare feet as she shimmied up the tree. The rough trunk scratched and covered her skin with sticky resin. She had no trouble holding herself steady while reaching out with one sturdy hand to unhook the back of her brother's linsey-woolsey shirt from a stout branch. "Hold still, critter," she said. Her brother snarled like a treed coon but did as he was told. As soon as he was free, he gripped the trunk and followed her lickety-split down the tree.

When Big landed on the ground with a thud, the first thing he did was to knock over Little as hard as he could. Little sprawled flat, then sat up, dazed.

"What'd you do that for?" Elizabeth demanded, shaking the pine needles out of her bright red hair.

"For crying like a girl," Big said and made a fierce face at his cowering brother.

Little rubbed his eyes with his dirty hand, stood up, and sniffed.

"Come on. Let's go." Big gave his brother another poke and bounded down the trail.

Little followed, running as fast as he could.

Elizabeth watched the two red-haired boys, who were nearly mirror images of each other—only one was a few inches taller and a few pounds heavier. Big and Little hooted and called to each other. For all their scrapping and clapper-clawing, they were the very best of friends. Big and Little ate together, played together, slept together. Once upon a time Elizabeth remembered that she and Martha had been that way, too. To her surprise, she felt sad to think of those long ago days. *Gone forever.* She shook her head as if to banish the odd memory. Then she picked up the bucket and started walking.

When she reached the spring, the boys were already dipping their grubby hands into the fresh clear water that seeped mysteriously from beneath rocks and pebbles at the foot of a giant oak. The burbling water made a shallow pool that was cluttered now with fallen leaves. Until last spring it had been the regular job of one of the settlers to keep the spring cleared of leaves and branches.

Big slurped a cupped handful of cold springwater. "Makes your teeth achey," he declared.

"Achey! Achey! Achey!" Little said and laughed. He splashed his brother. Big splashed back.

"Get away, you two!" Elizabeth said. She waded into the pool, leaned over, and cleared away the leaves. Slowly she dipped the bucket into the water. "You know what Barney Stagner would do if he found you splashing and messing in his spring?"

"Nothing," Big said triumphantly. "He won't do nothing. He's dead. He got his head cut off."

He made a slashing motion at his neck with his finger. "Shawnee did it."

Little took a step back out of the water. His mouth made a pinched O shape.

Suddenly, from somewhere nearby, came a bloodcurdling howl that didn't sound like a human or a beast. Elizabeth shuddered and dropped the bucket. The boys froze.

"A haunt!" Elizabeth cried. She looked every which way for a sign of the angry ghost, too frightened to remember the right finger motions or words that Parthena had taught her.

"GIVE ME . . ." the eerie voice shrieked. "GIVE . . . GIVE ME . . ."

Big's face was pale, even under layers of dirt. "What's he say?"

"Shut up and listen," Elizabeth hissed.

"GIVE ME . . . GIVE ME BACK MY HEAD!"

Big gulped. "Barney Stagner!"

"Run!" shouted Little.

Elizabeth jumped out of the spring. She scooped up Little under one arm and galloped down the path after Big. Not once did she look back. She was certain that the headless ghost of Barney Stagner was following them as they darted between the dark trees all the way back to the settlement.

Breathlessly Elizabeth and her brothers dashed past the tall wooden palisade, a fence of upright logs that surrounded the rude cluster of settlement cabins. They didn't pay any attention to the two stray dogs that chased after them. They didn't notice curious Mr. Feeny peering out his store window. They didn't hear Aunt Genevy, who leaned on her hoe in her garden. "You there!" she shrieked. "What you see? Not Cherokee I hope."

The children hurdled toward their cabin, but were stopped at the last moment from entering its warm, familiar safety by their father. William Poage, a short, chunky, swarthy-skinned man with a thatch of coal black hair, leaned in the doorway. His legs were stretched across the doorway so that the children could not wriggle past. "Whoa!" he said in a low voice. Big and Little screeched to a halt and tumbled together in a heap in the dust. "Baby's sleeping. All wild young ones stay out. Ma's orders."

"Daddy, we heared a haunt at the spring!" Elizabeth blurted. The babyish name she used to call her father had jumped to her lips unbidden. She clamped her mouth shut tight in case it might escape again.

Pa smiled. "Whose haunt?"

"Barney Stagner," said Big. He rubbed the place on his forehead where he'd bumped into his brother's head.

"That so?" Pa said, his smile fading. "Must have been a particular turrable haunt to scare you so bad you forgot the bucket. Your mother's waiting for that fresh water. We got a heap of things to get ready before we leave tomorrow."

Elizabeth buried one big toe in the dust. *The bucket!* Now she'd have to go back through the woods. What if she met with Barney Stagner's ghost again?

"GIVE ME . . . GIVE ME . . . GIVE ME!"

Elizabeth started, hearing that horrible, familiar voice. Her brothers jumped up and clung to their father. Pa let out a loud whoop. He wriggled free from Big and Little and pointed into the distance. "Here comes your haunt now!"

Skinny Martha teetered toward them carrying the heavy bucket filled with water. She managed a few steps before placing it on the ground again. Her hands free, she took from under her arm a piece of birch bark curled into a cone shape. She held this to her mouth. "GIVE ME BACK MY HEAD!" she called in an eerie, sending voice. She grinned mischievously. "Cowards! You should have seen how afeared you looked back there. Faces white. Knees ashaking. Just like slow wit Amos Feeny the last time he followed Elizabeth home clutching a bunch of mayapple."

Elizabeth felt her face flush. Even her ears burned. Martha had been sworn to secrecy about Amos.

"Martha, you skunked them good!" Pa said. He laughed and laughed.

"Elizabeth's got a heart burn!" Big taunted.

"Heart burn! Heart burn!" Little echoed.

Elizabeth gave her brothers a withering glare. "She called you cowards, too."

Furiously Big and Little barreled toward Martha. They jumped her. The three rolled and kicked and scratched in the dirt. "Big, I throwed you four times!" shouted Martha. "Why don't you stay throwed?"

Big scrambled to his feet, as if determined not to be beaten by a girl. He spit dust and head-butted his small, wiry sister. She sprawled forward, knocked off balance.

Pa cheered. Elizabeth scowled. She did not find her sneaky sister's practical joke or her comments about Amos the least bit funny. Secretly she hoped Big and Little would give Martha a black eye. Or better yet, maybe two.

"Wrasslin's over," Pa announced. His voice was stern even though his eyes still twinkled. "We got work to do. Need to find a first-rate forked limb of white oak. Any of you see a piece of a certain shape and bigness to make a pack saddle prong?"

"Me!" shouted Big. "I seen it. I seen plenty!"

"Me, too!" echoed Little.

"I'll find some perfect white oak for you," Martha said. She ran her fingers through her unruly black hair and smiled up at her father. "I always know where to find it, don't I, Pa?"

Pa smiled. "Big and Little, you can help, too. Let's go." He picked up his ax, which leaned against the side of the cabin. "When we get to Caintuck it'll be easy to find just the wood we need. Plenty of the best trees, plenty of game—land so rich and fertile makes you want to weep. No more worn-out fields, no more high prices for land, no more quit rents."

"Caintuck!" Little hollered.

Pa grinned. "That's right. Caintuck."

"Pa?" Elizabeth spoke up. "Can't I come, too?"

"Ma's got some special errand for you," Pa replied and winked.

"Yes, sir," Elizabeth said in a small, sad voice.

She watched Pa place the ax on his shoulder and gesture "Foller me." The boys leaped and galloped ahead. Martha took Pa's hand, then turned and gave Elizabeth a self-satisfied smirk.

Elizabeth struggled to smile. *Special errand.* She did not want to appear as disappointed as she felt. Deep down, she would rather go with Pa and the others into the woods. He always made their expeditions into games. Who could best imitate a whippoorwill? Who could be first to find a furry caterpillar or track down the den of a fox? As they walked along, Pa would tell them where to hunt a slender hickory sapling for a corn pounder sweeper or how to find just the right cane stalk to make a weaver's sleigh. He knew everything about the forest: what wood would float, what would bend, and what was best for a shoe peg. "Poplar's good for hewing and gouging," he always said, "but cedar's best for riving."

As the foursome headed into the trees beyond the cabins, Martha's sweet, clear voice shook the crimps out of Pa's favorite song:

"Violets in the holler
Poke greens in the dish
Bluebird, fly up
Give me my wish!"

Pa's distinctive lilting whistle sailed across the clearing in accompaniment. The happy duet made Elizabeth furious. She yanked up the heavy bucket so fast, water splashed on her skirt as she stomped into the cabin.

Ma looked up at Elizabeth from her stool in the corner where she sat at the spinning wheel. "You look like you got the weary dismals today."

"I'm fine," Elizabeth replied and plunked the bucket on the hard-packed dirt floor.

The spinning wheel whirred. Ma's right foot pushed the treadle up and down, a flat board attached to a crank that turned the spinning wheel that Pa had fashioned with pieces of oak. Two grooves in the edge of the wheel guided two belts, one turning the spindle, the other the bobbin that ran on the spindle. With her hands Ma skillfully twisted the flax yarn, feeding new fiber to the spindle so smoothly there were neither slubs or lumps nor thin, weak places on the yarn. With her left foot she rocked Mary's cradle. "Could have sworn I heard your sister rolling a song beyond the cabin just now."

Elizabeth nodded. She viciously twisted the hem of her wet skirt. "Yes, ma'am. And I don't mind saying I hate her singing nearly as much as I hate *her.*"

The whirring spinning wheel stopped. "You don't hate your sister. She's your blood. She's your kin."

Elizabeth shoved a bunch of frizzy red hair out of her eyes. *Ma can never understand.*

"Sit yourself on that bench." Ma set the spinning wheel whirring again. "Did I ever tell you the story of when you and Martha were wee babes lying in this very cradle?"

Elizabeth nodded slowly. *Not the wood tick story again!* Even though she had heard that tale a hundred million trillion times, she tried to act as if she wanted to listen. It wasn't every day that she could wheedle real talk from her mother. Ordinarily Ma was too busy bustling from garden to hearth to washtub. *Now that I can finally talk to Ma in private, why, oh why, do I have to hear about Martha?* Elizabeth picked up a rag and began scrubbing the trenchers with water from the bucket. *My sister the best friend stealer. The one who plays mean tricks and can't keep secrets. The one who wrestles like a boy and plays Pa's favorite and—*

"You listening?" Ma said.

Elizabeth looked up. "Yes, ma'am."

Ma cleared her throat. "The first wood tick that lighted on to you was quick plucked and killed on a book so that the omen might hold true that you'd grow up to learn to speak all kinds of proper words. But when Martha was just a wee babe, her first wood tick was killed on a clear-ringing bell, and that accounts for her fine singing voice. . . ."

Elizabeth wiped her arms dry with a scratchy

rag of woven hemp and glanced critically at the freckles that crowded the back of her hands, up her wrists. She had freckles on her face, too. Even Aunt Genevy's cobweb dew cure hadn't washed them away. *Course freckles aren't a problem for Martha.* "She's a Poage if ever there was one," Pa always said. The sun never burned Martha's skin. Her hair was straight, black, and thick like Pa's. She and Pa had the same black eyes, too. *Dark as water down a deep well.*

"You both have different gifts." Ma looked up at Elizabeth. "Didn't hear a word I said, did you?"

Elizabeth sucked in her bottom lip and bit it. "Yes, ma'am. Kind of. But what I was thinking was—"

"Yes?"

"We scarce look like sisters at all."

The spinning wheel whirled faster. "Big and Little with their red hair, same as you and me, before mine went gray." Ma glanced into the cradle. "Then there's baby Mary with the same black hair as Martha. That's how it seems to go: half the family light, half the family dark. Like mountains following valleys following mountains. . . ."

Elizabeth thought about mountains and valleys. *I still don't like Martha.*

"Each different, yet each one needing the other," Ma concluded, as if her explanation had made everything perfectly clear. "You must get along with your sister and stand by each other. Family's the most important thing in the world and don't you forget that."

"Yes, ma'am," Elizabeth replied halfheartedly.

Mary lifted her head. Her thick black hair bristled straight up like a fierce warrior's. She raised herself up in the cradle that Pa had made by hollowing out a log. Each end of the log cradle had a flat curved board to keep the bed from tipping over. Mary's little fists uncurled and pressed furiously against the sides of the cradle. She wrinkled her pink face and let out a terrific wail. Secretly Elizabeth thought her baby sister was as ugly as a mud fence dabbed over with toad frogs. But she never told Ma that. Ma seemed to love Mary with all her might.

Ma glanced down at the wide-awake baby. "I've got more flax to spin. We need to take as much as we can with us."

"I'll watch Mary so you can finish."

Ma stopped the spinning wheel. "My mind's

rambling like wild geese to the west. So many things to remember before we go. Pa said Mr. Feeny wants to see you at the store."

"Why?" Elizabeth asked. She lifted soggy Mary from the cradle. The baby squirmed and twisted in her sack-shaped, linsey-woolsey gown. She howled louder than ever. "I've got to change your hippin. You're a filthy mite, Mary."

"Don't know. Our account's paid up," Ma said absentmindedly. The spinning wheel began whirring again. "You'll have to take the baby along."

Elizabeth sighed. Expertly she replaced Mary's soiled diaper. "There. Good as new." Elizabeth hoisted her squirming sister on to her hip. She wished for once she didn't have to take somebody along on an errand. But Big or Little or Mary always seemed to need minding. Why for once couldn't Martha help instead of chasing off into the woods?

Just as Elizabeth was about to go out the door, Ma called to her again. "Now don't leave here looking like the hind wheels of bad luck."

"I ain't sad." Elizabeth frowned and jiggled Mary.

"Before all the commotion tomorrow, getting ready to go to Caintuck," Ma said, "I want to tell you. I want to tell you . . ." She paused as if her thoughts had escaped her again.

"What?"

"Honey, you know you is precious, don't you?"

Elizabeth gulped. Not since she was a little child could she remember Ma calling after her with such a mess of sweet, soft words. This unexpected attention made Elizabeth so bumfuzzled, she felt light-headed. She mumbled goodbye, hurried out the door, and holding Mary tight in her arms, loped happy as a fawn come springtime all the way to Mr. Feeny's.

Chapter 3

Elizabeth hitched Mary up on her hip and climbed the two log steps that led to the open door of Mr. Feeny's store. A flea-bitten dog lounged on the unswept puncheon floor in a pool of sunlight that came from the store's one window. The dog looked up briefly, scratched itself, and went back to sleep.

"Hello, Red," Mr. Feeny said, using his nickname for her. Mr. Feeny lay sprawled atop the counter with a sack of cornmeal beneath his head. This was his favorite place to read the *Virginia Gazette.* Since there was no more school and few customers, relaxing and reading were Mr. Feeny's main occupations these days. "Says here that British troops opened fire some place in Massachusetts. Forty-nine Americans killed, thirty-nine wounded. 'The sword is now unsheathed. Our friends are slaughtered by our cruel enemies.' " Mr. Feeny shook his head in disgust. "While those fellows back East are busy shooting at each other, we're afraid to go out at night in case some Cherokee decides to take our scalp."

"Yes, sir." Elizabeth watched him read. *Maybe he forgot he told me to come.*

After a few moments Mr. Feeny looked up at her again. He seemed startled to see her still standing there. Slowly he sat up and swung his long legs over the edge of the counter. A spare, large-boned man, he had keen gray eyes and shaggy white eyebrows. Carefully he folded the five-month-old *Virginia Gazette* in half and placed it on the shelf behind the counter where he kept the rest of his library: a stack of yellowing newspapers, pamphlets, two slim, worn books of poetry, a dictionary by Dr. Johnson, *The Grammar of Geography, The Pilgrim's Progress,* and Dilworth's *Grammar.*

Elizabeth scanned the remaining dusty shelves that ran along another wall. Jugs of whiskey stood in a row. A slab of rusty bacon, assorted costly pins and needles in papers, a bolt of much-admired calico, two watch fobs, and a half-dozen tins of snuff lay scattered here and there. Mr. Feeny's most valuable trade item was salt, a necessity every settler had to have to preserve meat. The salt was kept in a large covered barrel beside the counter. One bushel of salt was worth a good cow and calf in exchange. "How's business?" she asked in her most polite voice. *Maybe talk about the store will jar his memory why he told me to come.*

"Business is certainly not brisk." Mr. Feeny slid off the counter, which was a long table made of hewn logs. He lounged against the edge. "Can't get rum because of the British blockade. Luckily I've got plenty of home-brewed moonshine. Nobody's complained much yet. I hear you're getting ready to head out."

Elizabeth nodded, relieved to hear the conversation turn in a more familiar direction. "We leave tomorrow—as soon as the rest of the company gets here." She shifted her squirming sister to her other shoulder.

"Everybody in the settlement's sad to see your family go. Your pa's an ingenious contriver. Only person I ever met who could turn a rough block of wood into a fine polished bowl. And your ma's an accomplished spinner and weaver. Can't blame their wanderlust, though. All I hear these days is 'Caintuck, Caintuck, land of milk and honey.' Sounds like some kind of paradise."

"That's what Pa says, too," Elizabeth said and smiled. "Captain Boone told Pa, 'Best hunting, best land, best weather—best everything.' "

"Seems like wherever that Boone fellow goes, there's plenty eager to follow." Mr. Feeny removed his spectacles and rubbed the glass with his greasy shirttail. "It's nearly three hundred miles to Boone's settlement. Hope you make it safe and sound. Shawnee and Cherokee are on the prowl again. Hunters who came through last week said Indians burned Harrod's town. Not a cabin or a stalk of corn left standing."

Elizabeth nervously rocked her fretting sister. "Pa says we won't traipse along the trace any longer than we have to."

Mr. Feeny cocked his head. He made a silly face for Mary, who seemed fascinated by his shining spectacles. "This Poage looks bright as her big sister. Bet she'll learn to read just as quick."

Elizabeth bit her lip. "Pa said there's no school in Caintuck."

"Will be after a while."

"Not by the time we get there." Elizabeth took

a deep breath. "What if I forget everything you taught us? What if I forget how to read?"

"You won't." He cleared his throat and tapped his long, bony finger against the countertop. "The definition of a noun, Miss Poage?"

" 'The name of any Being or Thing perceivable either by the senses or understanding.' " She smiled with surprise that she recalled the class exercise.

"And here is something else, something special to help you practice." He pulled out a small green book that had been hidden beneath the bolt of calico. "This was packed in a crate of rifles from Philadelphia. Must have been sent here by mistake. I thought of you soon as I found it. 'Now, here's something Red would enjoy,' I said to myself. Would have given the book to Amos," he admitted, "but that boy's never going to learn to read, hard as I've tried to teach him. I got a book for him, too, though he never took much interest in it." He opened *The Pilgrim's Progress* and showed Elizabeth the inscription he'd written inside: "Amos Feeny his Book he may read good but God knows when." Mr. Feeny replaced *The Pilgrim's Progress* on the shelf.

Elizabeth eagerly examined the cover of her book. " '*Travels into Several Remote Nations of the*

World by Lemuel Gulliver, first a Surgeon, and then a Captain of several Ships.' What's a surgeon?"

"A kind of doctor."

"A doctor who knows how to sail a ship must be a very clever man," Elizabeth said and continued reading from the cover, "'*A Voyage to Lilliput; A Voyage to Brobdingnag; A Voyage to Laputa, Balnibarbi, Luggnagg, Glubbdubdrib, and Japan.*' What queer-sounding places. Do you think all the words are so long and cross-grained? I'm afraid I won't be able to finish something this difficult before we leave tomorrow."

Mr. Feeny chuckled. "The book's yours to keep."

"To keep?" Elizabeth licked her lips. She carefully turned the book over.

"Why the worried face? Don't you like it?"

"I do," Elizabeth said and handed the book back to Mr. Feeny. "But my folks won't let me keep something so valuable without paying for it proper. And I don't have anything to give."

Mr. Feeny was silent for a few moments. "Your pa's stubborn. That's the truth. Are you afraid he'll make you bring the book back?"

Elizabeth nodded. She looked longingly at the cover but did not dare open it again.

Mr. Feeny scratched the back of his head. "There is something I can ask you in return."

"What?"

"Some information. It's unlikely I'll ever go any farther west than the Holston. My traveling days are over. What I'd like you to do is tell me what you see on your way to Caintuck." Mr. Feeny took the book from her and opened it so that Elizabeth could admire the map and all the fine writing inside. Then he flipped to the back of Mr. Gulliver's book, where there were nearly half a dozen blank sheets of paper. "See this?"

Elizabeth nodded.

"Here's where you tell your story."

Elizabeth felt confused. "What should I write about?"

"Your journey. That's what Mr. Gulliver did. He wrote about what happened on his trip."

Elizabeth ran her hand tentatively across the book's smooth cover. Mr. Feeny's payment sounded difficult. "How will I send my writing to you?"

"When you're finished, tear out the pages and fold them just like you would a letter. Some traveler will tote your writing back East. There's always somebody coming through this way. Just write my name in big, clear letters: 'A. J. Feeny Mercantile.' Everybody knows me."

Elizabeth was silent for several moments, hoping she'd remember all of Mr. Feeny's directions.

"You're just a little fizzle sprout now," Mr. Feeny continued, "but you'll learn that one of the great satisfactions comes from knowing that the things we're doing now are going to linger on. One day you might want to read about your family's journey. Maybe when you're as old as Aunt Genevy."

That old? She could hardly imagine being so ancient. Then she thought about what Parthena had said in her letter. *Not to disremember me.* What if years and years passed and one day she forgot Parthena? What if she couldn't remember how they made their special mud pie ghost suppers, never once speaking to each other and all work done backward—walking backward and holding their hands behind them until all was ready for eating? And then at that precise moment how a supernatural sign would appear: a large white dog or two men carrying a corpse. Always something amazing and alarming. *What if I forget?*

"I guess you'll need this, too," Mr. Feeny said. He handed her a small envelope of powdered ink. In school she had seen him carefully pour the mysterious black powder into a small bottle of water. She watched in fascination as the powder bloomed and curled so that when he dipped his quill pen into the bottle, ink clung to the tip and left a mark just so on the paper. Like magic.

Trembling, Elizabeth held the little envelope in the palm of her one free hand. She wondered if her writing would ever look as beautiful as the lines of print inside Mr. Gulliver's book. "Thank you. Thank you, sir," she said.

Mr. Feeny smiled. "Seems to be no blockade on ink. Not yet at least."

Elizabeth placed the yawning baby on the counter for a moment. She slipped her shawl from her shoulders and wrapped the precious book and envelope of powdered ink inside. Mary whimpered and sucked her fingers. Elizabeth picked up her sister and the bundle and shuffled around the dog toward the door. "I best be going. Thank you again most kindly, sir."

"Don't forget what I told you. Write about the journey. Goodbye and God bless."

Chapter 4

Elizabeth hurried home, excited to show Ma her treasures. She paused quietly at the doorstep and peered inside. What she saw made her freeze. Beside the fire crouched her mother. Ma held a tiny shoe to the light for a moment, then tossed the precious object into the flames.

Elizabeth sucked in her breath. *Whose shoe?* Before she could ask, Ma leaned forward, her face in her hands. Her shoulders shook. Elizabeth felt dumbfounded, terrified. In all her life, she'd never seen Ma cry. *What should I do?*

Mary let out a whimper. Ma jumped to her feet and quickly wiped her cheeks with her apron. She cleared her throat and announced in her usual take-charge voice, "I'm just about finished. We can take nothing extra along."

The fire snapped and sizzled. Elizabeth tried not to look at the flames. She tried not to look at Ma's red-rimmed eyes. She felt embarrassed for spying. Still, she held the bundle close. *What if Ma says there isn't room for Mr. Feeny's book?* When her mother turned away to poke the fire with a stick, Elizabeth tucked the bundle between herself and Mary.

"What did Mr. Feeny want?" Ma asked. She hung the stewpot over the fire on a wooden pothook from a lug pole set across the inside of the chimney. Inside the pot was cornmeal mush—same supper they ate seven nights a week. Tonight they'd have mush and milk. When the cow went dry, they ate mush with maple syrup.

She's trying to keep from looking at me. She's trying to keep from showing me she was crying. "He just wanted to say goodbye," Elizabeth said, trying to think of something to cheer her. "He said everyone was going to miss you and Pa. That's all."

"We're going to miss everyone, too." Ma gazed off through the open door into the dark woods.

Don't cry again. Please don't cry. Elizabeth held the bundle and her sister even tighter.

"You can help me get supper ready," Ma said. "Your father's going to be up late working on that saddle. And we still have so much to get done."

When her mother turned toward the fire again, Elizabeth carefully lowered the bundle to the floor beside the cradle. She placed sleeping Mary in her cradle and covered her with a blanket. Then she grabbed the bundle and scurried up the ladder to the loft, where she slept with her brothers and sister. She hid the book and ink between her pallet and the wall.

"Elizabeth, you going to stir this pot?" Ma called.

"Yes, ma'am," she replied and hurried down the ladder.

That night, while Big and Little snored and she was certain Martha had gone to sleep, Elizabeth opened the book. She held it just above the loft opening. She could barely make out the words in the glimmer of firelight from below:

> CHAPTER ONE: The Author gives some account of himself and family. His first inducements to travel. He is shipwrecked, and

swims for his life, gets safe on shore in the country of Lilliput, is made a prisoner and carried up the country.

"Elizabeth?" Pa called. "I hear you prowling up there. Go to sleep."

Shivering, Elizabeth closed the book and slid back into her bed beside her sister. How did Pa always manage to see through the floorboards? She'd have to wait till they were on the trail to find out what happened to Mr. Gulliver. So many adventures! She hoped she and her family would not have as much trouble getting to Kentucky as he did getting to Lilliput.

She tucked Mr. Gulliver's story under the pallet. But when she closed her eyes, she saw Ma crying again. *Is that how it started with Parthena's mother?* Elizabeth pulled the blanket around her head. She'd think of something else. Something pleasant. *My own quill pen, my own bottle of ink.* In a few moments she was fast asleep.

The next day, as she did first thing every morning, Elizabeth crawled over her sleeping brothers and sister and peered out of the cracks between the logs of the cabin wall. "All clear!" she called to Pa on the floor below. He lifted the strong inside crossbar, raised the heavy latch, and opened the door, confident that no lurking Indians waited outside. Then he unbolted the wooden shutters of the cabin's only small square window.

"Big day," he said to Elizabeth as she climbed down the ladder from the loft.

"Yes, sir," she said. The cabin's dirt-packed floor felt cold on her bare feet.

"You see Mr. Feeny yesterday?"

"Yes, sir." Nervously Elizabeth watched sparks fly as Ma raked the glowing coals in the fireplace. "He just wanted to say goodbye."

Pa arched one eyebrow. "Told me he had something special to show you."

Elizabeth grabbed an extra wool shawl hanging from a peg on the wall and wrapped it around her shoulders. "A book. He found it in a crate of rifles. Nothing very interesting. I better get some more firewood," she said, hoping to change the subject. She rushed outside.

After the family finished eating, Elizabeth and Martha washed dishes. Then they began sorting into burlap sacks two precious pewter plates, one small dish, a stewpot, a bake kettle, a long-handled iron skillet with three legs and a gridiron for broiling, a long iron fork, a wooden ladle, and a corn grater—every dish and cooking utensil the family owned. Their next job was to fill gourds with pumpkin, oat, hemp, flax, and corn seeds. Most precious of all, according to Ma, was four pounds of cotton seed she wanted to take along.

Elizabeth and Martha spread clean quilts in the dry grass and rolled them into tight bundles. As they worked, Elizabeth considered telling Martha about Mr. Gulliver's wonderful book and Mr. Feeny's grand scheme for her to write about their journey. But when she recalled her sister's comment about Amos, she decided against the idea. *What if she ruins everything and tells Pa?*

"This quilt's rolling cater-cornered. See how crooked your edge is?" Elizabeth complained. "We have to make this bedding as small and tight as possible. Ma says we've got too much to carry already—what with only two packhorses."

"What difference does one crooked-edged quilt make?" Martha complained. "We'll just be unrolling it again come nightfall. When are the Callaways coming?"

Elizabeth shrugged. "Pa said this morning. Should have been here by now." She glanced quickly at her sister. Neither of them spoke, but Elizabeth knew they were thinking the same thing. *Indians.* She unrolled the quilt and began again. "Martha, you are as lazy as the hound that leans against a fence to bark. Are you going to help me or not?"

Martha groaned. "What if the Callaways never get here? Then what?"

"Then we have to stay put. Can't go all the way to Caintuck just our family. Isn't safe." *Better not mention Harrod's town. Martha might scare Big and Little just for jest.* Carefully she tied the quilt with a length of rope. "There. Now let's do the next one. You take that end."

"If Pa taught me to shoot," Martha said, "that would make two of us who could carry guns. Then we wouldn't have to tarry here no more. I could help protect us and get meat, too."

Elizabeth sat back on her heels and studied her scrawny sister. "One shot would knock you flat on your back. Besides, you're a girl."

Martha bristled. "What difference does that make?"

"Girls don't hunt." Elizabeth lugged the big featherbed from the fence rail. Stuffed with costly goose down and feathers, the fifty-pound featherbed was one of the family's most valuable belongings. She held one corner while Martha struggled to hoist the other.

Martha took a deep breath. "Pa said maybe—"

"Maybe what?"

"Maybe someday he'd teach me to shoot." Martha looked away, as if she did not want Elizabeth to study her face.

"Pa'll show Big and Little to shoot before he teaches you. And that's years away still. Me and Ma need your help. You've still got to learn to spin and—"

"Why can't I do both?" Martha interrupted. "Why can't I spin *and* shoot?"

Elizabeth paused to consider her sister's outlandish idea. "Because that's not the way things is done."

"Why?"

Elizabeth sighed. "Same reason when a rooster crows at night it's a sure sign of rain. Same reason laying a broom over a bed's bad luck. That's just the way it is, that's all. No reason why."

Martha sat back on her heels and crossed her arms in front of her skinny chest.

"You know Ma has a hundred chores need doing. Cooking, cleaning, sewing, mending,"

Elizabeth said, gentler now. "You can't spend all your time racing off into the woods."

"I can still be hoping, can't I? Maybe everything'll be different in Caintuck. It's a new country, ain't it?"

Elizabeth gathered up the quilts and stacked them like cords of firewood against the folded feather bed. "It's a new country," she said slowly, "but some things don't ever change."

Martha pouted. And for the first time, Elizabeth felt sorry for her sister. Had she been so completely ignorant when she was nine years old? She couldn't remember.

"What you staring at?" Martha demanded.

"Nothing," Elizabeth replied. Maybe her own dreams were just as foolish. She would never have a big sister, but that didn't keep her from wishing for one.

Suddenly, from outside the palisade, came a loud barking.

"That's Just," Martha said, instantly recognizing the family dog's distinctive warning howl. Years back, Pa had said the hound was "just a dog," and the name stuck.

More dogs in the settlement joined Just's chorus. Nervous barking filled the air. Martha looked anxiously at Elizabeth. What should they do? *Run and see who's coming or hide in the cabin?* Elizabeth sucked in her bottom lip. Unbidden, her earliest memory flooded back. *I'm holding Ma's apron. Women all around me are sobbing. Gunfire. Men shout. Someone carries in a bundle hanging from a pole. A bloody shirt. Noise and confusion—*

"Who's that?" Martha whispered.

"They're coming! They're coming!" a faraway voice shouted.

"Sounds like Big," Elizabeth said, filled with relief. "Better go see." She flew to the palisade gate with Martha close behind.

Big ran breathlessly toward them with Just close on his heels. His bare heels dug deep into the dust of the trail through the clearing. His face was bright red as if he had been running a long time. Bouncing behind him was flop-eared Just, a mixed-breed, general purpose dog. Gray speckled Just's muzzle. The old dog ranged all around, back and forth, scouting, sniffing—forever on the lookout for game or trouble. "The Callaways!" Big shouted. "I seen them. They're coming!"

"What did you see?" Martha asked.

Big paused, gulping for air. "People on horses.

Some growed up, some not. Couple of girls. They got some cows, too. And a fierce dog, but Just and I dodged him."

"Girls?" Elizabeth demanded eagerly. "A couple of girls? Are any *my* age?"

Big looked at her with disgust. "Who cares about girls?"

"Better go tell Pa, Big," Martha said and gave her little brother a shove. He dashed out of sight.

"Maybe one of the girls is eleven," Elizabeth said hopefully. "Pa never mentioned anybody interesting was traveling with us to Caintuck."

"Maybe he didn't know. Come on, let's see for ourselves." Martha grabbed Elizabeth's hand and tried to tug her down the path in the direction that Big had just come.

Elizabeth refused to budge. She couldn't. She felt too shy. Talking to Parthena had always been easy because she had known her all her life. What if she couldn't think of some clever way to greet these strangers? What if the Callaway girls decided she was offish and unfriendly?

"Don't you want to come?" Martha demanded.

"We'll see them soon enough. Let's wait here," Elizabeth begged.

"First you're excited they're coming. When

they get here, you want to duck under a rock. Stop being such a fly-up-the-creek and make up your mind."

"I'm staying put."

"Well, I'm going to see what they look like with my own eyes." Martha dashed away.

Elizabeth sat on a stump. She drummed her fingers on her knees. She tried whistling to pass the time as half the settlement joined her at the palisade gate. A string of horses trotted through the trees. In the lead strode a large meat-ax of a man with a ruddy complexion and a broad-rimmed brown hat. His beard was as wild as a stubble patch, and his hair hung to his shoulders. He waved and thundered, "Howdy!"

"Welcome, stranger, light and hitch!" someone shouted. "What took you so long, Colonel Callaway?"

A thin, sallow-faced woman with a slight limp came next. Elizabeth wondered if she'd stabbed her foot on a sharp, brittle stalk of cane. Four young men on foot followed her, each leading a pair of heavily loaded packhorses. One of the men had black skin. At the very end of the line, herding three cows along with switches, were two pretty girls who appeared to be slightly older than Elizabeth—perhaps fourteen or sixteen years old. They both had dark hair and matching blue calico dresses. The older one was a big-toothed girl with thin cheeks and flashing blue eyes. The other was slightly fairer and carried a bouquet of yellow maple leaves. Arms linked, they waved gaily at their greeters at the gate.

Elizabeth gulped. She watched, slack-jawed and amazed, as the Callaway girls whispered to each other and giggled. *Sisters. Absolutely perfect sisters.*

"Go on," Ma said, giving Elizabeth a little push. "Say hello."

But Elizabeth wouldn't budge. Her mouth felt as if it were filled with cattail fluff. What possibly could she say to such nearly grown-up girls? Surely they were as splendid as Parthena's young lady cousins who sat on riverbanks under shade trees eating ham and biscuits.

"Well, I'll not be so unfriendly," Ma said. She smoothed the kerchief tied around her head and called to the limping woman, "Proud to know you, Mrs. Callaway. Come and rest a while."

Mrs. Callaway looked at Ma and the rest of the crowd with critical, unsmiling eyes. "You got some clean water here? My sore foot needs bathing."

Ma nodded. "I'll get you a basin of the freshest water this side of the Blue Ridge. My name's Ann Poage and my husband's William. He knows Cherokee. Me and William and our young ones will be traveling with you."

Mrs. Callaway sniffed as if she were unimpressed. She jerked one thumb in the direction of the path on which they'd come. "That one of yours?"

Zigzagging down the path behind the Callaway group stumbled the unmistakable form of Martha, now covered from head to toe in thick, black swamp mud. In spite of her sorry appearance, she sang out in a merry voice.

"Come to me, my dear, and give me your hand
And let us take a social ramble to some far
and distant land
Where the hawk shot the buzzard and the
buzzard shot the crow
And we all ride around the canebrake and
shoot the buffalo-OOOOO. . . ."

"Martha!" Ma called. "What happened to you?"

"Callaway dog jumped Just. Then they both chased me into the swamp. Landed in some mud. No harm done. They got one stupid hound," Martha said. Her face was so blackened with mud that when she smiled, her teeth appeared as white as pumpkin seeds.

"That hound's not stupid," Mrs. Callaway replied indignantly. "That hound is one of my husband's finest hunting dogs."

Martha scratched her mud-caked head. "Could have fooled me. Don't seem to notice the difference between a girl and a critter."

Mrs. Callaway clucked and turned to Ma. "Your cabin? Where is it? I'd like to rest my foot."

"Right this way," Ma said. She led Mrs. Callaway to their cabin.

Elizabeth felt terrified as the two Callaway girls came closer. She kept her eyes lowered and marked a line in the dirt with her toe.

"You got a name, girl?" the older one demanded.

"Elizabeth."

"What might your age be?"

Elizabeth cleared her throat. "Eleven or thereabout."

"Big for your years. Would have thought you

at least thirteen," the older girl said with obvious disappointment in her voice.

Elizabeth felt her face flush. She slouched forward a bit so she didn't seem so tall.

"I'm Betsey," the older girl announced. "She's Fanny."

"That your sister?" Fanny demanded. "The one covered with mud?"

Elizabeth nodded shyly. "Her name is Martha."

"Muddy Martha," Fanny said and burst into laughter.

Betsey giggled. Pretty soon, both of them were hooting and holding their sides. Elizabeth couldn't help herself. She started chuckling, too. Her sister *did* look ridiculous.

Martha did not think her new name was funny. Angrily she stomped away. She was not seen again until suppertime, when the only dirt remaining on her could be seen on the back of her neck, behind her ears, and lodged in the folds of her soggy, damp dress.

To the surprise and pleasure of everyone in the settlement, a fiddle had been brought along on one of the Callaway packhorses—all the way from Virginia. The Callaway slave, whose name was Enoch, knew how to play all manner of reels. The wiry, unsmiling young man, who seemed to be perhaps twenty years old, stood on a stump and knocked out the rhythm with the heel of his boot as he played the tunes: "Jenny put the kettle on; Molly blow the bellows strong; we'll all take tea" and "Leather Britches full of stitches" and "Billy in the wild woods."

There were just twenty or so folks—young and old—living in the settlement. Everyone came to the beat-down spot in front of Mr. Feeny's store. A bonfire was built, and Mr. Feeny brought out some jugs of whiskey, and soon the whole settlement was lined up, couples facing, young and old, linking arms and dancing till midnight.

Elizabeth had never heard such marvelous fiddle music. She danced with Pa. She swung round arms with Martha and Ma. Big and Little jumped and clapped and sang along. The three young men who'd come with the Callaways were eager to dance, too. The one called Daniel Drake was a short, shifty-eyed fellow with a scalp belt and two fancy pearl-handled pistol guns he wore even while he danced. David Wright was older; he came from Massachusetts. He had a wisp of a yellow beard and smelled strongly of skunk. Moses Austin was a jolly, round young fellow, who seemed to enjoy demonstrating the latest Virginia reel. Elizabeth watched as Betsey and Fanny pranced and twirled like accomplished dancers. Only their mother, who had hurt her foot, seemed resigned to sit on a log with Aunt Genevy.

"Play some more!" Austin shouted. "We want to dance all night, for tomorrow we're on our way to be rich, landed men in Cain-tuck-ee!"

Enoch mopped his forehead with a red kerchief.

"Play, Enoch!" bellowed the colonel.

"Give the man a rest," Pa said. He hoisted a mug of whiskey for Enoch, who gladly took the refreshment.

Enoch wiped his lips. He pulled the bow back and forth across the strings while the colonel called: "Nappycot and petticoat and the linsey gown, if you want to keep your credit up, pay your money down!"

Elizabeth smiled. She watched Pa swing round Ma. She watched her brothers dancing with Martha. The fire leaped and hissed. In the circle of light the dangerous dark woods and mountains beyond the settlement seemed very far away.

At daylight the next morning the settlement became a flurry of activity as the horses in the pack train were saddled and loaded. Colonel Callaway, Pa, and the other men clumsily strapped double-girthed packsaddles on to the reluctant horses. They cinched the breeching tight enough so that the saddles wouldn't slip. Around each horse's neck was placed a bell hung on a wide strap.

"Tie those clappers," Pa told Elizabeth. "We don't want Indians five miles away hear us coming."

Elizabeth struggled to avoid being bitten or stomped on while she secured the bell clappers with ropes. She knew that when they camped that night and the horses were hobbled, the bells would be "opened." The ringing bells would make it easier to find the grazing horses in the woods.

"Hold still," Pa hissed at the swaybacked mare, one of two horses the family owned. He strapped on either side of the horse's saddle a pannier, a large basket of woven thin splints of wood. Elizabeth and Ma quickly filled the panniers with rolled bundles of clothing, blankets, and seed corn. They stowed away the cooking utensils.

Wooden trenchers, piggins, and noggins were stuffed in sacks and loaded on the top. Room had to be found for the precious bag of salt, gunpowder, and lead for molding bullets. When their supply of johnnycake, jerky, ham, bacon, and cheese were gone, the travelers would be dependent on wild game. "If Big and Little get tired, they can climb in and rest in these baskets," Pa said.

When Big heard this, he pouted. "I can walk to Caintuck," he announced.

Pa chuckled. "We'll see."

"Safe journey," Mr. Feeny said and slapped Pa on the back.

Aunt Genevy's old hands trembled as she gave

Ma a bunch of dried rattlesnake weed in case they came upon any copperheads. "It's a good thing you're leaving today," Aunt Genevy said. "If you started out tomorrow, it'd be Friday. Friday's never a good day to begin a journey."

Big and Little raced back and forth along the pack train, hooting and hollering. Just barked and pranced. Elizabeth placed Mr. Feeny's book, her ink bottle, quill, Parthena's letter, and her only change of clothing inside her linsey shawl and carefully tied together the four corners. She slung the bundle over one shoulder and watched Martha pace barefoot in the dirt with a long, straight branch. Every so often she stopped and probed the ground with the stick. *Thump! Thump! Thump!*

"Why you got your eyes shut?" Elizabeth demanded.

"So I don't have to look at you," Martha said and made a face. "To see a red-haired girl in the morning of the day you are going on a trip brings bad luck."

Elizabeth stuck out her tongue at her sister.

In the distance Colonel Callaway bellowed, "Heading out!" Elizabeth looked all around for Fanny and Betsey. Perhaps she could walk with them. *We'll walk along and talk about whatever older girls talk about.* She spotted the Callaway girls in their matching blue sunbonnets with limp brims that nearly covered their faces. "Morning," she said in a slow, shy voice.

Betsey and Fanny leaned toward each other and hissed loud enough for Elizabeth to hear, "Cohee hair!" They shrieked with laughter, grabbed each other's hands, and ran down the trail.

Elizabeth frowned and tried to smooth her frizzy curls. She broke a long slender stick and switched it back and forth in the air. *Zip-zip-zip.* Blue mooed. "Get along!" she shouted angrily. The cow shuffled along with a bundle of Pa's tools strapped on her back. Chinkapin trundled past and crashed through a holly patch. It took much coaxing and shouting to convince the sow to join the end of the long, single-file line of travelers. *At this rate, we'll never get to Caintuck.*

The other settlers waved and called. Some whooped. Some wept into their aprons. "Goodbye!" Elizabeth shouted to Mr. Feeny. She coaxed Blue and Chinkapin along the trail that led out of the settlement. She trained her gaze straight ahead and tried not to glance backward one last time. By now she hoped their neighbors were going about their business again and weren't watching the pack train disappear. Hadn't Aunt Genevy told her that if you watched a traveler out of sight, you'd never see her again?

The path followed the river, which sang a kind of lonesome goodbye song against the rocks. Walking behind slow-moving Blue and Chinkapin gave Elizabeth plenty of time to think. What would she write when she had a chance? *"Everything looks the same. Same dark trees. Same wide river."* Nothing worth mentioning yet. She wondered about what Mr. Feeny had told her. What if nothing exciting or worth writing about happened on their trip? What then?

Chinkapin and Blue grazed on what little greenery they could find along the trail. Since there was no room to tote oats or extra feed, the cow nibbled cane. The hog munched acorns and mast. Chinkapin wasn't particular and ate whatever was available, including a sleepy copperhead strewn across the path. The hog squashed its head with her hoof. She picked up the writhing snake with her sharp teeth, threw back her head, and swallowed it whole.

Every so often Elizabeth broke a twig from a

clean, woody bush, peeled the bark away, and chewed the sweet, white insides. As she walked, she looked for sweet dark wild grapes, hickory nuts, walnuts, and chokecherries that the birds had not yet found. But always she watched for any sign of Indians—an imprint of a moccasin in soft dirt, an odd doe's bleat. Pa had told her if she saw or heard anything suspicious to warn the others by putting her two fingers in her mouth and whistling loud and shrill.

"Hello!" Elizabeth called to Just. All morning the busy old dog steadfastly prowled back and forth, up and down the line of travelers. When Just reached Elizabeth at the end of the line, he'd stay a few minutes, sniff along behind the sleepy cow and pig, then dash to the front as soon as he heard Big's shout or Pa's holler. "You're going to walk your legs off," Elizabeth called after the dog. He didn't seem to care.

They walked on and on through the shadowy trees. Elizabeth's stomach growled. She felt relieved finally to smell the smoke of a campfire and something cooking up ahead. That meant they'd be stopping to eat a noonday meal of crisp johnnycake Ma had fried and packed the night before. Maybe there'd be some jerked meat, too.

The men shouted at the balking horses, who were being hobbled so they wouldn't run off while grazing.

"You're as slow as Christmas coming!" Betsey said when she saw Elizabeth, the last to arrive. Betsey perched with her sister on a fallen branch, hunched over, chewing a piece of tough, dried venison. Elizabeth wondered if she should feel grateful that the Callaways had finally spoken to her that day. She smiled as friendly as she could, but the girls went back to chewing their meat.

A campfire blazed. Big and Little roasted pieces of jerked venison wrapped on sticks. The Calloways' slave, Enoch, sat on his haunches beside the three other men. He quickly scooped roasted meat into his mouth and washed the gritty, tough meat down with a cup of water. Like the other men, he ate silently, intensely, as if he were afraid someone might take his food.

Ma handed Elizabeth a chunk of johnnycake half an inch thick and a cup of water dipped from the river. Elizabeth was so hungry, she gobbled the food standing up. Because the Callaway girls seemed particularly unfriendly, she chose to rest beside Martha, who had stretched out on a pile of bright, fallen leaves.

Martha rolled over and sat up on one elbow. She looked at Elizabeth, who pulled a gob of prickers from her skirt. "You got much more book-learning than me. Maybe you know," Martha said slowly. "What happens if we just keep walking?"

"What do you mean?"

"If we never stop moving west, where will we end up?"

Elizabeth shrugged. She'd never considered what might exist beyond Boonesborough, the settlement named after Captain Daniel Boone.

"What's past Caintuck?" Martha demanded.

Elizabeth tossed the prickers as far as she could. "I don't know. Where you get such a crazy idea?"

Martha rolled over on her back again and gazed skyward. "I bet past Caintuck's the edge of the world."

"Edge of the world? What kind of foolishness is that?"

"Makes sense to me. Pretty soon if you go far enough, you come to the edge of the world. That's the place where you can't go no farther. All that's left is a straight-down cliff so steep you can't see bottom."

Elizabeth sucked in her breath through her lips. The idea of the edge of the world gave her the chills. She wished she could ask Mr. Feeny if such a place existed. He'd know.

"Must be a place like that," Martha insisted. "Land can't go on forever, can it?"

Elizabeth shrugged. She had never read about what lay beyond Caintuck, and she'd never pondered such questions before. She glanced curiously at her sister, who was studying a daddy longlegs that marched across her foot. *What goes on in that head of hers?*

Above them an enormous flock of passenger pigeons suddenly darkened the sky. The noisy birds were flying south. Their loud cries sounded almost weary. Winter was coming. *What if we don't make it to Caintuck before the first snow?*

"Line up! Head out!" Colonel Callaway called.

Elizabeth stood up and brushed the leaves from the back of her skirt. "I wouldn't worry too much about the edge of the world. A long way off shouldn't give you call to fret."

"Maybe," Martha said. She stretched and started walking. Elizabeth rounded up Blue and Chinkapin, and the group headed down the trail.

By midafternoon the travelers had wandered

into a valley. Here the hills opened out half a mile wide and a mile long. Everywhere were more tall, dark trees. It wasn't until they'd nearly come upon the crude log station that Elizabeth realized they'd reached some form of civilization. The station was a group of log houses connected by a high wooden wall to form a crude palisaded fort. The wall was made of close-set posts, ten or twelve feet high.

The station, she judged, was smaller than most she had known back on the Holston. This one looked to be barely twenty or thirty steps square, and a hastily built two-story cabin stood at each of the four corners. Trees and underbrush had been cleared around so that the settlers could look out in all directions, giving little cover to Indians who might try to fire inside. A tall, thick wooden gate swung open on creaking leather hinges.

"Welcome, welcome!" called a small, thin man in breeches and a remarkably colorful deerskin hunting shirt with the word *Liberty* emblazoned on the back. The loose shirt had no buttons and reached halfway down his thighs and lapped over the full width of his body in front. The sleeves were generously wide. A fancy fringed shoulder cape with bright red beads and dangles hung about his shoulders. At his waist was tied a brilliant green woven belt. On his head was a plaited straw hat decorated about the brim with the long black and white tail of a skunk. He introduced himself as Captain John Anderson. "I'm a Ring-tailed Roarer who happens to own this blockhouse. Built it myself. This is the last station before you reach Moccasin Gap, gateway to Indian country. Try some of my whiskey, will you?"

"Don't mind if I do," Colonel Callaway replied. "Better warn you I'm a moderate drinker. Limit myself to a single quart at a sitting. More than that might lay to my head." He let out a loud bellow of laughter.

Captain Anderson pushed wide open the palisade gate and waved them in. At the center of the station was an open area dotted here and there by freshly cut stumps. A small fire still smoldered where someone had been burning brush and roots.

Elizabeth herded the stubborn sow and cow away from the remains of a corn patch. Her brothers practiced jumping from stump to stump. Mary cried. Ma handed her to Martha, who looked none too pleased. Meanwhile, Elizabeth helped open the bells on the horses. Enoch and the other men unloaded the gear for the evening. As Elizabeth worked she listened to Captain Anderson talking to Pa.

"Where you headed?" Captain Anderson asked.

"Boonesborough."

Captain Anderson pulled out his corncob pipe and pushed a wad of strong-smelling black tobacco into the pipe. "Had some folks just like yourselves come through, maybe a week ago."

"On their way to Caintuck?" Pa asked eagerly.

Captain Anderson stuck a long stick into the brush fire. He watched the end flare. Then he lit his pipe and took a long, slow draw. Acrid smoke blew from his lips. "No, these folks were headed east. Cherokee convinced them to return. Not the first I've seen turn back. Boone and his family only got as far as Walden Creek two years ago. Course you probably already heard what happened to his young son and that other poor boy . . ."

Pa turned and spoke in a low voice so that Elizabeth couldn't hear what he was saying.

"Elizabeth!" Ma called. "Help gather up some firewood. I need two buckets of fresh water at least. Take your brothers so they stay out of mischief."

Elizabeth sighed. She wanted to hear more about what happened to the people who had fled Caintuck. She knew Ma wouldn't wait, though. Elizabeth switched the long branch in the air and herded the pig and cow to the far end of the enclosure, where she saw Betsey and Fanny. Enoch did their milking chores. They had plenty of time to rest. Elizabeth watched with envy as Fanny braided her sister's long brown hair. *Martha would never let me do that.*

Elizabeth picked up the two heavy wooden buckets that hung from a wooden yoke. The yoke fit around the back of her neck. Each bucket hung at her side from a thick rope. "Come on, Big. Come on, Little," she called to her brothers, who were punching each other in the dirt. "You help gather firewood."

Together they walked outside the palisade to the little spring that bubbled up beyond a spot where Captain Anderson had dumped old bones, broken crockery, the remains of barrels, and part of a wagon wheel. Big and Little wandered about, gathering kindling and small branches. Elizabeth bent over and filled one bucket, then the other. Suddenly she heard the whickering cry of an owl. She froze. Then she whistled and called softly, "Big? Little?"

"What?" Big said, his face pale even under the grime. He grabbed his brother by the back of his shirt and motioned for him to be silent. Instantly Little obeyed.

Elizabeth tipped her head in slow motion in the direction of the blockhouse. Big knew what to do. He held tight to his brother and the two took off in a gallop toward the open gate. Elizabeth gulped. She scanned the trees and listened hard.

No movement. No sound.

Nothing.

Yet she knew. Somewhere deep in the darkening woods someone was watching them.

Elizabeth's legs shook as she stood up with the two heavy buckets yoked about her neck. As fast as she could, she sped barefoot across the stubbled ground. The water sloshed and the yoke bit into her neck. She did not slow down or stop until she arrived breathlessly inside the blockhouse and shoved the gate shut behind her with a loud *Crash!*

"What'd you see?" Colonel Callaway demanded. He grabbed his gun and signaled to the four young men and Enoch to take positions with loaded rifles.

"Not sure," Elizabeth said in a quavering voice. "Heard something. Indian owl call."

Colonel Callaway wiped his brow with his large bandanna. "You aren't making this up to get attention, I hope. I knowed girls who did such a thing." He glanced over at his whispering daughters, who huddled together a few yards away.

Pa stepped forward. Anybody could see he was angry. "Colonel, Elizabeth ain't lying. She's not Tuckahoe like you folks from old Virginia. Elizabeth's pure Cohee—born and raised in these western hills. She knows what it means to be watchful."

Elizabeth felt pleased and surprised. *Pa's standing up for me.*

Colonel Callaway did not reply. He simply signaled to the other men and announced in a booming voice loud enough for any Cherokee on the other side of the wall to hear that they would have sentries posted through the night.

"Ambush?" Captain Anderson said in a slurred voice. He stumbled from his cabin with red, bleary eyes.

Pa shook his head. "We're keeping watch, though. Heard something."

"Ain't nothing compared to Caintuck. No, sir. In Caintuck you'll hear buffalo bellow from the treetops." Having made this pronouncement, Captain Anderson wobbled his way back to his bed.

Elizabeth shuffled toward the campfire, where her mother was slowly coaxing the flames with more sticks of wood. She placed the buckets on the ground and slumped onto a log to rest. *I know what I heard.*

"You all right?" Ma asked.

Elizabeth nodded. She held her elbows in each hand and looked about the blockhouse. The walls looked thick enough. But she could see light between the logs. She shivered when she realized that anyone who wanted to attack them had only to wait until the morning when they were on the trail to Caintuck again.

That night the gate was kept shut and the horses were hobbled inside the palisade walls in case of an Indian raid. The Callaway family slept on blankets on the blockhouse cabin floor. Pa and the other men took turns standing guard in the blockhouse windows.

Elizabeth lay beside her snoring sister, next to the fire. The evening was moonless and cool. No wind blew. She wrapped herself in a blanket and a cloak, but she could still feel the hard, cold ground. An owl hooted. Her eyes flashed open. Try as she might, she knew she couldn't go back to sleep. She looked around and saw that no one else in her family was awake. Big and Little were curled like two spoons against each other. Mary lay in Ma's arms.

Slowly so as not to wake anyone, Elizabeth removed Mr. Feeny's gift from the bundle with her cloak. She opened the precious book, holding it to the firelight so that she could just make out the wavering words about Mr. Gulliver's early life and the disastrous storm that destroyed his ship and forced him overboard:

> . . . I SWAM AS FORTUNE DIRECTED ME, and was pushed forward by wind and tide. I often let my legs drop, and could feel no bottom: but when I was almost gone and able to struggle no longer, I found myself within my depth; and by this time the storm was much abated. . . .

Elizabeth recalled the time she accidentally fell into the Holston and how cold and frightening the water felt when it crept up around her neck and how she flailed her arms back and forth and choked until Pa waded in and saved her. Was that what Mr. Gulliver felt like, too?

> . . . I WALKED NEAR A MILE before I got to the shore, which I conjectured was about eight o'clock in the evening. I then advanced

forward near half a mile, but could not discover any signs of houses or inhabitants; at least I was in so weak a condition, that I did not observe them. . . .

What a strange journey! Mr. Gulliver's travels seemed as filled with danger as her family's. She had heard Pa say there would be no more houses, no other settlements for nearly three hundred miles after they left the blockhouse. "We'll be on our own," Pa said, "and God help us."

Shivering, Elizabeth drew the blanket around herself. *This is as good a time as any.* She slipped the small stoppered bottle from her bundle. She stood up and walked carefully to the bucket of drinking water. She dipped the bottle into the bucket. *Glug!* Martha rolled over. Elizabeth held perfectly still until she heard more snoring. Then she tiptoed back to her sleeping place beside the fire. She gingerly tore a tiny corner from the envelope Mr. Feeny had given her. She held it over the bottle of water and tapped it slowly. The powder with its wonderful mysterious black smell swirled into the water.

She turned to the first blank page at the back of the book. *What should I write?* She glanced at her sleeping mother and baby sister. A trace of a smile crept across Mary's face. Ma said when a baby smiled in its sleep, an angel was talking to it. Elizabeth wondered what the angel might be saying to Mary. She dipped her quill into the ink and wrote:

Septmber 13, 1775

Set out Early with packhorses for Caintuck. Traveled to block House our last Shelter. Enoch doesnt play his fiddle Tonight. I askd him why. He Says hes to sad and lonly missn his wife and babe in Virginia he never will see agin.

Elizabeth wondered what Enoch's baby was called. How would it feel to travel so far away that a person might never see their newborn babe again?

Suddenly Mary's smile vanished. Her face wrinkled up and she let out a terrific howl. Ma fumbled, half-awake, and rose up on one elbow to hush her. In Elizabeth's haste to hide her book beneath the blanket, she knocked over the ink bottle. She watched in horror as the ink quickly soaked into the ground. Every last drop—gone! Frantically she tried to scoop up the precious dark puddle with her hand, but succeeded only in staining her hand.

"Elizabeth, what's the matter?" Ma whispered.

"Nothing," Elizabeth lied. Sadly she scooped dirt over the remains of the ink. *Gone. All gone.* She stared at the back of her hand.

"Go to sleep," Ma said. "We have a long day tomorrow."

Elizabeth pretended to hunker down on her blanket, but she kept her eyes open. When Mary was finally quiet again, Elizabeth slipped the book from under the blanket to make sure it had not been splashed by spilled ink. When she flipped to the back of the book, she read what little she'd written. *Five lines.* She sighed. What would she do with no ink—and the journey just begun? Brokenhearted, she stoppered the empty ink bottle and hid it and the goose quill beneath the blanket. She closed her eyes and fell asleep.

The next morning the company of travelers awoke to a cold, mizzling rain. The mountains were concealed in clouds as Pa and the others rounded up the packhorses. Elizabeth milked Blue and handed Ma the pail. Ma divided what little there was into four wooden bowls and mixed it with a spoonful of cornmeal mush that she had cooked over the fire. The children and the rest of the company huddled as near as they could to the fire as they ate.

"I'm so hungry, I could eat a bull, and it bellering," Martha said in a muffled voice with her apron over her head. She scooped the contents of the bowl directly into her mouth.

"Wished we had clabber," complained Big, whose favorite dish was sour milk, curds, and whey.

"You Cohees!" Mrs. Callaway exclaimed disdainfully. She nibbled on a piece of stale clapbread, a small cake of unleavened dough that had been baked in the fire on a flat bakestone. "If you was a Tuckahoe, you'd only feed such disgusting sour milk slops to your cattle."

Fanny and Betsey giggled.

Ma gave Mrs. Callaway a dangerous sideways look as if she meant to say something hurting. Instead, she kept her voice in her pocket and remained silent.

"What's a Cohee?" Martha whispered to Elizabeth.

"Somebody like us—from border country this side of the mountains," Elizabeth said in a low voice.

"What's a Tuckahoe?" Martha demanded.

"Lowland Virginians from out east."

"All Tuckahoes have slaves?"

Elizabeth shook her head. She shoved some more mush into her mouth and gave her sister a warning look that meant for her to shut up. She didn't want Martha's question to set Ma off about the evils of owning slavery. Not when the morning was going so badly already. Elizabeth peeked at Fanny and Betsey, who primly finished the last of their bread and dabbed the corners of their mouths with handkerchiefs from their apron pockets.

Colonel Callaway called to the men to head out. The gate swung open. Captain Anderson waved a bleary goodbye, calling, "Be wary of Indians! Keep your powder dry."

The long line began winding through the dark, drizzly woods. Colonel Callaway was followed by Drake and Wright. Austin and Enoch herded the Callaway cattle. Elizabeth and her family brought up the rear. Packhorse hooves clomped against the slippery, wet stones. Bridles jangled against closed bells. Dogs barked. Ma handed Mary to Elizabeth to carry for a while since the baby was too fussy to travel in the pannier.

Elizabeth balanced Mary on one hip. She looked longingly ahead to the place she knew

Betsey and Fanny were walking, companionably sharing a blanket to try to keep dry. *Lucky! They don't have to tote any screaming baby.*

Elizabeth wrapped her shawl tight around her head and shoulders with her baby sister inside. She hoped that the hidden book would not get wet—either from the rain or from Mary. "Sooey! Sooey!" she called to Chinkapin. The sow crashed through the undergrowth.

Only Martha, who led Blue by a rope, seemed in high spirits as she walked along with Elizabeth. "Wouldn't it be fine tonight to roast a fat turkey for our supper?"

Elizabeth nodded. Her eyes darted here and there in the dark shadows between the trees, ever watchful. There had been no more signs of Indians all night, which had caused Austin to complain at breakfast, "I'd rather have rest than safety."

"Those two Callaways are the most unfriendly critters I ever met." Martha coaxed the stubborn cow to walk faster. "Mrs. Callaway told the colonel she was sorely disappointed not to be traveling with a better sort. What she mean by that?"

Elizabeth shrugged.

"I heared Mrs. Callaway complain she had to

leave her chiner behind and how was she supposed to drink her tea. I thought tea was slops—ain't that what Pa says?"

Elizabeth let out a long breath. She rubbed her ink-stained hand on her skirt, though it did no good. "Tea's for persons of quality who don't labor. Fancy folks. That's what Parthena told me and I believe her."

Martha seemed to mull this answer over in her mind for several moments before speaking again. "That Callaway woman's fancy, sure enough. And she's some sharp talker. Ain't nothing she don't know and ain't nobody she can't mock down to the point of nothing."

Elizabeth did not reply. It bothered her that Mrs. Callaway thought her family so inferior. What distressed her even more, however, was the fact that Betsey and Fanny seemed to agree completely with their mother. *Maybe that's why they won't talk to me.* Being seen with Muddy Martha was undoubtedly only making their opinions of her worse.

"What's ailing you?" Martha demanded when Elizabeth refused to speak to her.

"Nothing," Elizabeth replied. She saw Fanny and Betsey look back at them and giggle. Elizabeth hid her inky hand. "Leave me alone," she told her sister.

With a hurt expression Martha slowed her gait. Elizabeth bustled ahead. The rest of the morning she avoided Martha as best she could.

The group traveled two miles before fording the North Fork of the Holston River. As soon as they left the Holston for good and began traveling up higher into rough hill country, Elizabeth felt at last that they were making their way through new territory. The newness seemed frightening and fascinating at the same time. The trail twisted and turned, barely wide enough to let a loaded horse pass between the thick trees, up through Moccasin Gap, the only passway through the Clinch Mountains.

When they reached the gap, Elizabeth turned briefly and looked east. The hills rolled away black upon blue upon gray. She had no idea where the Holston settlement was among the unfamiliar peaks and valleys. Her other life seemed very far away.

They trudged on all morning, stopped briefly for a noon meal of cold johnnycake and jerked meat. When Mary finally fell asleep, Elizabeth placed her wrapped in a blanket in the pannier. The travelers walked west toward the Clinch River, up the valley of Little Moccasin Creek and down the valley of Troublesome Creek. At times the valley stretched on either side away so gently. It wasn't until they reached Troublesome Creek that they found their luck had changed.

On either side of the Troublesome, mountains rose up dark and steep and menacing. What little was left of the trail seemed to disappear.

"You sure we're headed the right direction?" Pa called to Colonel Callaway. The company stopped and looked up the steep creek bed pocked with pools and rocks and ledges and the twisted remains of fallen trees and driftwood.

"You seem to forget I helped Boone cut this trail. Got me ten pounds ten shillings—enough to buy four hundred and twenty acres of good Caintuck land—for my troubles. You listen to me. I know where I'm going," Colonel Callaway said with obvious irritation. "We follow the creek bed to the Clinch River ford."

The packhorses balked. They slipped and plunged and shifted along the wet rocks. Their hooves hit the sharp rocks and rang out in the steep valley. Elizabeth scanned the trees that rose up on each side of them. *A perfect place for an ambush.* She tied her apron tight around herself so that her precious bundle of belongings bobbed safely around her waist. She took each brother by the hand and helped him climb over treacherous moss-covered boulders. "Come on, boys! At least the rain's stopped."

"Tired!" Little cried.

"Shut up," Big said.

Elizabeth and her brothers climbed up the creek bed in a hurried, reckless fashion until they needed to stop to catch their breath. They leaned against a shattered log.

Suddenly both horses Enoch was leading reared and pitched their packs forward. The spooked horses struggled up the steep embankment and disappeared over the ridge.

"Hold on!" Colonel Callaway cried. Drake and Wright scrambled to grab the reins of the other horses before they dumped their loads into the pools of water. Austin scrambled up the ridge, but he wasn't fast enough. The horses were gone. After nearly half an hour of terrible frustration, the rest of the pack train was under control.

"Three powder gourds broke and a whole wallet of corn burst!" Pa said angrily and swore a long string of colorful oaths. "And now here we are sitting pretty, just waiting to be massacred."

"Then best you pray, Mr. Poage, not swear."

Mrs. Callaway retied her sunbonnet tightly, as if to better shield her ears.

"I've no time to pray, dammit," Pa replied.

Colonel Callaway ordered Austin and Enoch to follow him on foot to capture the runaway horses. "Meantime, rest of you stay and put things in order," the colonel said. "Poage, Drake, and Wright stand sentry. We'll be back before nightfall."

Ma handed Mary back to Elizabeth and began to collect what handfuls of corn she could. With help from Mrs. Callaway and Enoch, they began repacking precious gourds of seeds. "Keep these boys out of the way," Ma told Elizabeth in a flustered voice.

Elizabeth found a flat rock along the bank and dragged her two brothers and baby Mary up to the spot. She untied her apron, pulled out the book and opened it to chapter one.

"What's that?" Big demanded.

"A story," Elizabeth explained. "Sit still and listen and I'll tell you what's happened so far to Mr. Gulliver, who got swept from his boat into the deep ocean and swam to an island."

Big and Little fidgeted and poked each other but managed to find enough space on the rock to sit cross-legged. They listened in fascination as she read aloud:

". . . WHEN I AWAKED, it was just daylight. I attempted to rise, but was not able to stir: for as I happened to lie on my back, I found my arms and legs were strongly fastened on each side to the ground; and my hair, which was long and thick, tied down in the same manner. I likewise felt several slender ligatures cross my body, from my armpits to my thighs. . . ."

"What's a ligature?" demanded Martha, who had crept nearby.

"A rope maybe. I don't know. Stop interrupting," Elizabeth said with irritation. She shifted sleeping Mary to her other leg, which was tingling and cramped from holding still so long.

"I COULD ONLY LOOK UPWARDS; the sun began to grow hot, and the light offended my eyes. I heard a confused noise about me, but, in the posture I lay, could see nothing except the sky. In a little time I felt something alive moving on my left leg, which advancing gently foward over my breast, came almost up to my chin—"

"I know what's on him," Big interrupted with a triumphant grin on his face. "Hairy spider."

"Ain't no spider. Bet it's a gray squirrel," Martha said with authority.

"Shut up the two of you if you want to hear what happens," Elizabeth said. She wondered if reading the book was such a good idea with so many interruptions. But she cleared her throat and kept going.

". . . WHEN, BENDING MY EYES DOWNwards as much as I could, I perceived it to be a human creature not six inches high, with a bow and arrow in his hands, and a quiver at his back. . . ."

"An Indian!" Big cried.

Martha smacked her brother hard. "Ain't Indians six inches high."

"How high's that?" Big asked.

"Big as my hand maybe," Martha said. "Be quiet, will you, so she can keep going."

Elizabeth continued reading:

"IN THE MEAN TIME, I felt at least forty more of the same kind . . . I was in the utmost astonishment, and roared so loud, that they all ran back in a fright; and some of them, as I was afterwards told, were hurt with the falls they got by leaping from my sides upon the ground—"

"Elizabeth! Martha!" Ma called.

Martha licked her lips. "Don't stop. What else does it say?"

Elizabeth rubbed her eyes. Now both legs were asleep. "We've got to help get ready to move on. Ma wants us."

"Just a little more. Read a little more," Big pleaded.

Elizabeth smiled. She had not expected her brothers and sister to find Mr. Gulliver's book so fascinating. Before she could slide from the rock, cradling Mary in one arm, Martha stopped her. "Do you think," Martha whispered, looking about over her shoulder, "we might find such little people with arrows and bows on our way to Caintuck?"

"If I found a little man like that, I'd put him

in my pocket," Big said bravely. "He won't shoot me then."

Little laughed and clapped as if his brother were the most clever person in the whole world.

Elizabeth rolled her eyes. "It's just a story. See?" She held out the book for them all to see. "Just words on paper. It never really happened, don't you know?"

"But it *sounds* true," Martha said, her head cocked to one side. "You're going to keep reading, aren't you?"

Elizabeth took a deep breath. She flipped open the book and let her thumb run across the many pages. When she came to the last page, she noticed her five lines about their own journey. She looked up at her hopeful sister. Suddenly she had an idea. "I'll read more," Elizabeth said slowly, "if you do something for me."

"What?" Martha asked, as if pleased to strike any kind of bargain.

"Find me a mess of pokeberries."

Martha looked at her as if she were crazy. "Pokeberries? What you need those for?"

"That's my secret," Elizabeth said and smiled. "You find them and I'll keep reading."

Chapter 7

september 14

We Start Early & travel this Day along a verey Bad hilley Place riddled with caves but Pa says no time to explore. way cross one creek whear the horses almost got Mired Some fell in & all wet their loads we cross Clinch River & Betsy and Fanny shreek so pritty when they git carried piggy back across by Enoch, even though the water comes barely to their knees and they were in no danger of drowning we travell till late in Night & camp on cove creek When we git here Colnl Calloway beats Enoch for loosing a pack he sends him to look for it but when Enoch returns he says animals got everything and he gits beat again

In the dim light of dawn the next day Elizabeth sat in a secluded spot beneath a tree, as far away from her brothers and sister and the other travelers as she could hide. She reread what she had written the night before, even though she could think of so much more to write. How the Clinch River had looked—black and cold—and how it smelled hanging in the air, like something rotting and musky and mysterious. How wet and dark and slippery the rocks were—especially where the trees' shadows kept them hidden from sunlight all day. And how the crossing place wasn't much more than a shoal in the river formed by an exposed ledge of rock. Somehow crossing that river made her feel as if she were leaving home forever. Now they were on the other side of the Pine Mountains and she couldn't see the Holston anymore. They'd be following buffalo traces, pounded hard and deep and wide by herds searching out salt licks.

She lifted the bottle of ink and held it up to what little light there was. The campfire Austin and Enoch had built crackled and popped. She could tell there was only a small amount of ink left, even though she had carefully squashed every one of the pokeberries Martha had found and poured the juice into the little bottle. The swipes of color the berries made reminded her of a storm cloud in spring or the color of early-morning sky overhead. She shut the book and stretched her legs. Her back was stiff from sleeping on the cold, damp ground. Yesterday she had walked all day long and her feet and legs were sore and tired. Today they would walk even farther.

"Elizabeth!" Ma called.

Elizabeth sighed and stood up. "Coming." She hid the book inside her apron. Her stomach growled. She longed for something hot and tasty—flapjacks and syrup or maybe a piece of soft, white bread smothered in honey. Anything except cornmeal mush or another piece of meat.

"You need to milk Blue, though I don't know how much you'll be able to get from her. She's been walking so far, so long, I'm afraid she's going to go dry," Ma said. She looked tired as she handed Elizabeth the bucket. "Most of our cornmeal got wet crossing the river. I hope your father or one of the other men has some luck hunting today, or we'll have some hungry days soon."

Elizabeth fumbled with the bucket and dropped the book.

"What's that?" Ma demanded.

"Nothing." Elizabeth picked the book up in a hurry and dusted off the cover.

Ma gave her a tell-me-the-truth look.

"Mr. Feeny gave it to me before we left."

"Let me see."

Elizabeth handed her the book and bit her lip. She watched nervously as her mother thumbed through the pages. Ma couldn't read, but she had a powerful respect for books. "Why'd you ruin something so precious with this?" Ma demanded, pointing to Elizabeth's words on the back pages. "You know you ain't supposed to write in a schoolbook."

Elizabeth cleared her throat. "Mr. Feeny told me to write there."

"In this perfectly good book?" Ma asked in disbelief.

"He told me to write about our trip. He said so we wouldn't ever forget."

Ma squinted as she studied the letters Elizabeth had made with pokeberry ink. "Not much here."

Elizabeth took a deep breath. "Yes, ma'am. But we just started out."

Ma looked up at her and smiled. Elizabeth felt relieved. "That wood tick omen proved right, just as I said it would," Ma said. "See all these proper words you can make?" She gave back the book.

Gratefully Elizabeth hid it in her belt and picked up the bucket. She strode off into the edge of the camp to look for the cow. She heard the familiar *tong-tong-tong* of the cowbell and found Blue nibbling a few tufts of dried grass. She tied the cow's bridle to a small sapling so she wouldn't wander too far. Then she squatted on the ground, trying her best to keep the mosquitoes out of her face as she milked the cow.

Tweet! Tweeeeet! Elizabeth looked up. Fanny and Betsey stood nearby, each playing a hollow whistle made from a willow branch. "You seen our cow?" Fanny asked.

Elizabeth shook her head and kept milking. "She lost?"

Fanny nodded. "Enoch's been sent to look for her. Hope he don't get scalped."

"Or run off," Betsey added. She played a little tune.

Elizabeth wondered if Enoch had run away

before. But she decided not to ask, just in case doing so might put the Callaway girls into an evil humor so they stopped talking to her. This was the longest either of them had ever paid any attention to her, and she felt nearly giddy with delight. *What should I say?* Elizabeth longed to say something so engaging that the girls would linger longer. "That's a pretty song," she said finally.

"Your sister taught us," Betsey said. Her slender fingers moved up and down the little whistle. "She's very musical."

Elizabeth's shoulders sank.

"Martha made these whistles for us special," Fanny explained. "Cut them with her knife."

Elizabeth frowned. "Nothing hard about making a whistle. In the spring even Big knows how to get some small pieces of young sourwood and cut a sprout and rub the bark loose with another sprout and pull that bark off. Then all you do is cut a mouthpiece where you blow into it. Fix a piece to go back down the end to plug it up. Nothing special about making a whistle that I know."

Betsey and Fanny played a little tune. Then they laughed and whispered together.

"What happened to your hand? Looks all

black," Betsey said, then added in a sly voice, "What you trying to do, look like Enoch?"

"We saw you talking to him like he was somebody," Fanny added. "Papa don't like that, you hear?"

Elizabeth felt her face redden. She stood up quickly and untied Blue. Then she picked up the milk bucket, which was only one-quarter full, and delivered it to her mother.

Ma stirred the last of the cornmeal into water. The smoke smarted Elizabeth's eyes. She tried not to be angry with Betsey and Fanny. *Maybe they're just trying to give me a friendly warning. For my own good.* Somehow thinking these things did not make her feel any better.

"You seen your brothers and sister?" Ma asked. "We'll be eating soon."

"I'll go find them," Elizabeth replied. After a long search she rounded up her brothers, who had been hiding among the trees. They galloped around her, straddled on long branches that they pretended were horses. "Slow down!" she said. "It's time to eat. Where's Martha?"

"Whoa!" Big called. He pulled up on the imaginary reins. "With those stupid girls by the creek."

Elizabeth crossed her arms in front of herself. *That Martha! Stealing friends again.* "What are they doing?"

"I wanted to trounce some more frogs, but they said no," Big replied.

Elizabeth rolled her eyes. She could just imagine the faces of the sensitive Callaway girls when they watched her brothers catapult a frog through the air on the end of a stick that had been clobbered with a rock. "That's nasty."

Big screwed up his face as if he were thinking very hard. "Frog don't care. Feels like flying to him."

Elizabeth sighed. "What were the girls doing by the creek?"

"Playing something stupid. Floating leaves for boats. How should I know? They told us to go away and leave them alone. You want to see the bow and arrow Pa made me and Little with a piece of hickory and some whang leather?"

"No," Elizabeth replied absentmindedly. She craned her neck to see if she could spot Martha and the Callaway girls. She wished they'd invite her to play floating boats.

"Elizabeth!" Ma called.

Elizabeth sighed. Why did she have to work

while Martha was out having a good time along the creek bank? It wasn't fair. "Martha! Come on! Breakfast's ready," Elizabeth called.

Her sister appeared pale faced, running as fast as she could. It was the fastest Elizabeth had ever seen Martha come when she was called. On her heels, running just as fast, were the two Callaway girls. Their expressions were equally alarmed.

"Where's Pa?" Martha demanded breathlessly. "We just seen fresh moccasin tracks."

"You sure?" Elizabeth asked.

Martha nodded. "I know what they look like."

"We saw them, too," Betsey said. She and her sister shivered like quaking aspens.

It wasn't long before Colonel Callaway and Pa inspected the muddy creek bank and studied the tracks that ran along the shore and disappeared into the water. "Cherokee all right," Pa said when they returned to the rest of the group huddled beside the fire. "Probably made last night while we were sleeping."

Elizabeth gulped.

"Wouldn't the dogs have heard them and started howling?" Moses asked nervously.

Colonel Callaway shrugged. "Some Indians is

clever. They know how to put a spell on a dog that makes it speechless."

"How many Indians?" Wright demanded.

"Hard to tell," Pa replied. "Sometimes they walk in each other's footprints. So you can't tell what their number is."

"Might be hundreds," Fanny said fearfully. "What should we do, Papa?"

"We're going to be watchful," Colonel Callaway said. "We have good guns, good powder, and we could beat them if we could get first fire. Unless of course they was greatly over our number. The main thing is that we have a good resolution."

"Well, I wished we'd come upon a whole swarm of Indians," Drake announced loud enough for everyone to hear. "I want so bad to have the chance of killing them. I know I could kill five myself. Why, I can shoot. I can tomerhawk and I can make use of my butcher knife and slay them just like that."

Pa shook his head. "Young fellow, you got a lot to learn. You don't go around picking a fight with no Cherokee for the fun of it."

"I don't aim to have fun," Drake replied darkly. Callaway's dog wandered past, and he gave him a rough pat. "When I was back on the Clinch River, we fed three Indians to the dogs to make them fierce watchdogs. They bristled up and quarreled as they ate. Maybe we should—"

"I think," Ma interrupted, "we'd best finish what little we have for breakfast and then pack up and move on as soon as we can. We need meat. Somebody's got to go out and hunt as we move along or there'll be nothing to fill these children's bellies come suppertime."

"She's right," Colonel Callaway said. He slapped Drake's back. "There'll be plenty of other chances for glory."

Elizabeth herded her brothers and sister to the campfire. She held Mary in her lap and ate quickly. With each swallow Big and Little nervously scanned the surrounding trees.

The company packed the horses and set out across the ford of Stock Creek, where the hard mountain travel began. The path followed the creek in a torturous, steep climb over the north end of Stock Creek Ridge. Elizabeth tugged and pulled on Blue's bridle to convince the cow to take step after step up the steep incline. Chinkapin halted every few feet and rolled its eyes as if it might expire any moment. "Get along!" Elizabeth shouted. She tried not to look down the steep way they had just come. Her feet slipped on tumbling rocks, and she found it hard to move very quickly without stubbing her toes.

Meanwhile, Martha tugged and pulled Big and Little up the steep path. Whenever Little started to whimper, Martha sang a song to keep the boys walking in step. Elizabeth found, however, that singing to Blue and Chinkapin did not have any effect at all.

As soon as they finally reached the highest point, Horton's Summit, Elizabeth turned and looked back toward Purchase Ridge. The clouds had lifted and the blue of the mountains faded back into gray then to gray-blue then to black. *So many mountains!* She felt discouraged. Every which way she looked, she saw more hills, more valleys. *How far till Caintuck?*

When the entire company had assembled near the summit, gourds filled with water were passed around. Austin and Wright sat on logs. Drake and Enoch stretched out on a ledge and looked out over the endless expanse of trees. No one spoke.

"We'll rest a while before we head down," Colonel Callaway announced finally. "It's going to be as steep going as it was coming. While some of you rest, Enoch and I are going to take a shortcut up Devil's Race Path to hunt. We'll meet at Little Flat Lick."

"Be careful, my darling," Mrs. Callaway said in a sullen voice.

Colonel Callaway tipped his hat. He and reluctant Enoch disappeared down the other side of the hill.

Elizabeth leaned against a tree with her brothers nearby lying on their backs, gazing up at the sky. She hoped they'd find something to eat—perhaps a couple nice fat turkeys. Stealthily she slipped the book from her apron and opened it, hoping that her brothers wouldn't notice.

"Read!" Little commanded.

"Yeah," Big agreed. "We want to know what happens next."

Her brothers inched closer so that she could smell their greasy hair and their unwashed faces, and it was clear they were not going to allow her to read her book to herself in peace. "All right," she said and began to tell how Mr. Gulliver managed to free his head and one hand a little by pulling hard on the strings that had tied his hair to the ground. The tiny creatures shot arrows at him.

". . . I FELL A GROANING with grief and pain, and then striving to get loose, they discharged another volley larger than the first, and some of them attempted with spears to stick me in the sides; but, by good luck, I had on me a buff jerkin, which they could not pierce. . . ."

As she described how Mr. Gulliver lay still and how the little people stopped firing arrows, she noticed Martha sidling closer and sitting on a rock, listening intently.

". . . I HEARD A KNOCKING for above an hour, like people at work; when, turning my head that way, as well as the pegs and strings would permit me, I saw a stage erected about a foot and a half from the ground. . . ."

The little creatures had built several ladders as well, Elizabeth explained. And in time their leader mounted up on the platform and made a speech and then commanded that Mr. Gulliver be fed.

> ". . . SEVERAL LADDERS should be applied to my sides, on which above an hundred of the inhabitants mounted, and walked towards my mouth, laden with baskets full of meat. . . . There were shoulders, legs and loins shaped like those of muttons and very well dressed, but smaller than the wings of a lark. I ate them by two or three at a mouthful, and took three loaves at a time, about the bigness of musket bullets. . . ."

When Elizabeth looked up from her book, she noticed that Fanny and Betsey had taken a seat nearby as well. Their whistles lay on a nearby rock, unused. Betsey leaned forward with her elbows on her knees. Fanny cocked her head to one side. For the first time Elizabeth felt a kind of power. She could read. Martha couldn't. She smiled. At last she had the Callaway girls' attention. *Maybe now they'll let me be their friend.*

Later that afternoon the group made its way down the steep hill into a little valley situated in a bowl between the hills. Little Flat Lick, Pa said, was nothing more than a commonplace marshy field with a spring. What set it apart were the spring's minerals that caked the surrounding soil. The salty-tasting ground was said to attract game from miles away.

"How will we know when we find Little Flat Lick?" Elizabeth asked her sister as they walked along. The trace seemed to wander aimlessly between low marshy places, any one of which looked like the lick where Colonel Callaway had told them to meet him.

"Pa will find it," Martha said. But Elizabeth did not feel so sure. The colonel was the only one among them who'd ever been this way before. He'd told them, "Keep to the three-notched trail." But how were they to know which way to turn when the hatchet marks on the trees seemed to disappear suddenly?

Crack! A shot rang out flat. Elizabeth froze. Martha held her breath. They knew the difference between the sound of an Indian's less heavily loaded gun and the louder recoil of a settler's rifle.

"The colonel!" Drake shouted. And the line of travelers and horses ahead of the girls began to pick up speed.

"Think he's right?" Martha demanded.

Elizabeth shrugged. She licked her lips and hoped Drake knew something they didn't. *Maybe dinner won't be long.*

As soon as they came through the pines and headed into an open meadow, Pa called the group to an abrupt halt. Just howled and barked.

"Now what?" Martha whispered.

Elizabeth pointed beyond the stand of cane. "Indians," she said in a quavering voice.

"What they doing?"

"Can't tell," Elizabeth said. She peered at the group that stood beside something large and brown sprawled at their feet on the ground. Two men chanted in voices just loud enough for her to hear.

Meanwhile, Drake struggled to pull his rifle from the pack saddle. Wright and Austin primed their guns afresh and put two bullets each in their mouths in case there was a fight. When Drake raised his gun and took aim, Pa grabbed the rifle. "Don't be a fool," Pa said. "They're apologizing to the spirit of the buffalo."

"What for?" demanded Drake.

"For killing it so they can eat. Seen it plenty of times. It's a Cherokee ritual," Pa said. "Now, see how they've raised their hands to greet us? They don't mean any harm."

"I say shoot them," Drake replied.

Wright and Austin grunted in agreement.

"You don't know who else might be in those trees," Pa said between clenched teeth, motioning to the tall stand of oaks beside the meadow. "They've got a woman and child with them. It's a hunting party, not a war party. Put the rifle down before you get us all killed. Just!" Pa clapped his hands together and motioned for Just to come back and behave.

Reluctantly Drake and his two companions did as they were told. Pa instructed the group to remain where it was. He handed Ma his rifle, then walked slowly toward the Cherokee with his empty hands in the air. Elizabeth held her breath. The older Cherokee man raised his hand in greeting and gestured to the carcass. He kept his glance lowered as he spoke to Pa. Elizabeth wondered what they were talking about.

"What did they say?" Austin demanded when Pa returned.

"They invited us to dinner," Pa said, grinning.

Ma's face was pale, but she didn't say anything.

Betsey whimpered, "Where's our papa?"

"I don't want to eat with no Indians," Fanny agreed.

Mrs. Callaway put her finger to her lips to shush her daughters. "What do the savages want in return?"

"A gun repair, which I agreed to do," Pa said. "They've got a nice fat buffalo, and they're planning on building a fire and cooking it. I suggest we not insult them and join their feast." He gave

Drake a warning look. "And I suggest we use our best manners."

Big and Little hid behind Elizabeth as they approached the clearing. All their lives the boys had been told at night, "Lie still and go to sleep or the Shawnee will catch you." And now here they were face to face with a real Indian. They refused to peek around to look at their hosts, who included two men, a woman, and a young girl about Martha's age.

The woman, who wore a colorful kerchief around her head, quickly cut up the buffalo into sections, skewered a large piece with a long, straight stick, and set it over a blazing fire on two forked sticks. In a large earthen pot simmered sour corn broth. The two men lounged nearby. One wore a buckskin hunting shirt and a cap made of cloth with two red tassels hanging down, one on each side of the head with a long tail hanging down in back. The older man's calico shirt was trimmed up with silver brooches and armplates. Over his shoulders was flung a broadcloth capote, a long overcoat with a hood, the kind that Elizabeth had seen soldiers wearing.

Although the men could not speak much English, they seemed delighted to show off for Austin and Wright their two beaded shot pouches and long rifle that had been decorated on the wooden stock with various mysterious daubs of paint and carvings.

Pa unloaded what few blacksmithing tools he owned and went to work on the Indians' rifle. Drake kept his distance and spoke to no one. He watched suspiciously as the two Indians delighted in twirling Ma's spinning wheel. When they made signs that indicated they'd liked to trade the spinning wheel for two of their horses, Ma refused as politely as she could. With help from Pa, she told them, "No, thank you, sir. This article is not for trade." After that, Ma kept the spinning wheel near her even as she and Mrs. Callaway set out the wooden trenchers on a blanket spread on the ground.

As the sun set and the light faded, the air filled with the delicious roasting aroma of cooked meat. The activity involved in getting ready to eat seemed reassuringly familiar to Elizabeth. Just as she and her sister had regular cooking jobs on the trail, so did the Cherokee girl. She carried an armful of firewood and dumped it beside the fire. She glanced quickly at Elizabeth and then looked away as if she were frightened. The girl wore a calico dress exactly like her mother's. The dress reached to the middle of her legs. On her feet were soft deerskin moccasins decorated with beads. Her hair was braided and wound in wreaths, turned up and fastened on the top of her head with a silver brooch.

"What's your name?" Elizabeth asked as bravely as she could. She bent over to help stack the wood.

The girl nervously rubbed one finger over her top lip. For a moment Elizabeth thought she saw a smile.

"She don't know English, I expect," Fanny said, who stepped closer, her arm linked in her sister's. Fanny seemed to be studying the shy girl, who quickly retreated to the safety of the older Indian woman's presence. "Your father teach you any Cherokee?" she asked Elizabeth.

Elizabeth shook her head.

"Don't get too friendly," Betsey advised in a low, confidential voice.

"Why?" Elizabeth asked.

Betsey leaned closer. "They might take you captive."

Elizabeth gulped and shot a quick glance at the Indians.

"And white captives held for any length of time come to look just like Indians," Fanny said. "After a while they don't know their own name or their people's, and they look as much like an Indian for color and for dress as an Indian."

Betsey cleared her throat. "When we was living at Fort Patrick Henry, there was these two children brought back from the Shawnee. They'd been captured as babies and lived with the Indians ten years or more. Can you imagine? They wouldn't have a thing to do with their own rightful parents. Didn't recognize them. They just wanted to go back into the woods and live with the savages again. Their father cried out aloud and fell down on the floor, bewailing his condition. Said he, 'My cheldrin is Indians! My cheldrin is Indians!' Ain't that right, Fanny?"

Fanny nodded solemnly.

Elizabeth looked again at the group gathered at the campfire. She took a deep breath and wondered if what the Callaway girls said was true.

That evening the buffalo haunch was quickly eaten. The rest of the buffalo meat was cut into strips and set on sticks to smoke above the smoldering fire. Every time one of the dogs tried to steal the meat, the Cherokee girl threw a rock at it. Filled now with an enormous dinner, the travelers sat around the campfire in a contented silence. Martha kept her brothers beside her. The three children were so full from their big meal, they could only stare sleepily into the fire.

How strange! Elizabeth looked around the flickering light and could hardly believe that there they were, sharing an evening campsite with the people who they had been taught to believe were their very worst enemies. Pa picked his teeth. He took a long pull from a pipe and passed it to the Cherokee man in the red calico shirt, as if doing so were as natural as the activities of any other evening's campfire. Only Drake wasn't convinced of the Indians' friendly intentions. He leaned against a tree, as far away as he could from any of the Indians, and cleaned his fingernails with his enormous knife, watching, always watching.

Elizabeth decided that this encounter was the most exciting thing to happen so far on their trip. Carefully she slipped the ink, quill, and book about Mr. Gulliver from beneath a blanket. She sat at the very edge of the circle of light and struggled to draw a picture of the Indian family.

She jumped with surprise when she felt someone holding her by the shoulder.

When she looked up, she saw the Cherokee girl, intently staring down at her drawing of her mother and father and uncle. The girl pointed, as if in awe of the likeness. Before Elizabeth knew what was happening, the girl grabbed the book from her and held it close to her chest.

"Please," Elizabeth pleaded in a desperate voice. "Give it back." She held out her palms and motioned. Nervously she glanced over at Drake, who kept his rifle primed and ready beside him—ready for any kind of excuse to begin a fight. Elizabeth gulped. Gunfire was the last thing she wanted to start. "Let me show you," she said to the Cherokee girl. She held up the quill and ink bottle to the light.

Curious, the girl sat down beside her. Not once did she let go of the precious green book. "See?" Elizabeth said. She dipped the quill point into the little bottle and held it aloft. The girl studied the quill. Elizabeth put her hand on the book while motioning with the quill.

Little by little, the girl let go of the book. Elizabeth opened the book to a blank page and drew a rough portrait of the girl, complete with braids and silver broach and moccasins. The girl smiled. Elizabeth tore the page from the book and handed the picture to the girl. She smiled wider and admired the pokeberry marks on the paper. Quickly Elizabeth hid the book beneath her.

The Cherokee girl motioned to Elizabeth and handed her the page with the drawing. She pointed to the quill. Elizabeth dipped the pen into the ink bottle again. She drew a hog. She drew a passenger pigeon. She drew a horse. The horse's head was a bit too large and its body was a bit lumpish.

The girl examined the poor horse and said something in Cherokee. She laughed. Elizabeth couldn't understand what she said, but she thought she was probably right. The horse *was* rather sorry looking. "Kind of swaybacked," Elizabeth admitted, pointing at the horse.

"Swayback," the girl said, grinning.

They both laughed.

Chapter 9

September 16

When we wake up, Indians are gone. Frost early and cold. Just cant be fownd. I call and call. Betsey says Indieans Eat dogs. I dont believe her. Colnl Calloway Comes as we're about to brake camp. He did not shoot anything. The newz is very bad and he is furious. While he was hunting, Enoch wandered off with his horse and never came back. He called Enoch but he was very scarce. He's taken the other end of the Road and run away. Probably back to the Settlments. A search party has gone to look for him. If they do not find Enoch, perhaps at leest theyl Find Just. Steep climb over Powell Mountn thru Kane's Gap, four miles Strait down the other side. My feet's blistered bad and Mary won't eat

"Get up now. We've got to keep moving," Elizabeth whispered the next morning after she searched the woods around their campsite for Just. There seemed to be no sign of the old dog. She gave Big and Little a gentle prod. The two boys sat up, and their hair stood up spiky and greasy. They rubbed their eyes.

"You find him?" Big demanded.

"Not yet," Elizabeth said, trying to sound hopeful. "I'm sure he'll be back soon. He knows where to find us."

Nearby, Mary fretted and whimpered. Ma said she had thrush. Her mouth was sore with yellow blisters and she refused to nurse. Elizabeth worried how long she could go without food. Her little cheeks were pinched and the inside of her mouth was covered with yellow pussy blisters. She didn't howl with the kind of ferocity that was her custom. Ma tried everything she knew to rid the baby of the ailment. She placed a lock of Mary's hair into a hole in a tree. She tried spooning rainwater from a stump into her mouth.

She let a stallion snort in Mary's face. Nothing seemed to work.

"Only cure for thrush I know," Mrs. Callaway said, "is to get the baby to drink water that has been tossed in a stranger's right shoe from heel to toe three times. Or try giving that child blood from a chicken."

They had met no stranger on the trace and they had no chicken. "Aunt Genevy'd know what to do," Ma said in a low, sad voice only Elizabeth could hear. And for the first time Elizabeth was homesick for the Holston settlement, the last place she had felt safe. Along the trace there were no houses, no stores, no midwives—nobody who might know what to do to help them. They had to keep moving, forever westward, and hope that Mary would be all right.

Martha stood at the fire and divided four equal portions of meat into four trenchers for their breakfast. The children ate quickly, silently. Ma sat on the ground with Mary lying on her lap. She tried to squeeze a few drops of broth dipped in a rag into Mary's mouth. The baby would have none of the broth and began whimpering again.

"Stop!" Little demanded. He clapped his hands over his ears and shut his eyes, as if doing so would eliminate Mary's distress. Elizabeth and the other children listened helplessly and said nothing. Their sad eyes went everywhere except to one another. Elizabeth ate hurriedly and began to clean up the trenchers.

The packhorses, now only nine in number, were loaded. Since Colonel Callaway's departure with Drake and Wright to search for Enoch, Pa had been leading the group west. The colonel had promised to meet them at Wallen Ridge or possibly along Powell's Valley, where he promised that there would be plenty of game. The trace followed the creek bottoms and crisscrossed back and forth across the waterways. The only good thing about this part of the trace, he'd said, was that it was level and would become broader and more wide open as they traveled west. On one side rose up the hills of Wallen Ridge, on the other stood Powell Mountains.

Pa called to the tired company to begin the journey once again. "Come on, now! Let's get moving." He strode down the dark, misty trail with his rifle over his shoulder, leading the two packhorses. Next came Ma, carrying Mary. Mrs. Callaway followed, her foot now wrapped in a rag. Austin took bouncing steps as he walked along, balancing his rifle in the crook of his arm. His head swiveled left and right, searching the trees. At the end of the line straggled Elizabeth and her brothers and sisters and the Callaway girls.

Little tugged on Elizabeth's petticoat. "I want Just."

"He'll come back," she told her little brother. "You know how he likes to wander when he catches scent of something." Deep down, she knew it wasn't like Just to disappear for this long—nearly two days. What if he were hurt? What if he had been stolen by the Cherokee? They couldn't stop and look for him the way Colonel Callaway was searching for Enoch. Just wasn't as valuable as a slave, Pa had explained. "Now run along with your brother and pick up plenty of acorns along the way."

Little and Big ran ahead.

"I miss Just, too. He's sure a fine watchdog," Martha said, shaking her head sadly. "I'd sleep better if he came back."

"How do you think we feel having a father gone? That's much worse than missing a dog," Fanny said and sniffed. Since the departure of Colonel Callaway and Enoch, more work fell on the shoulders of Fanny and Betsey. Neither of them was accustomed to doing much in the way of labor. They complained when their mother told them to help with the packing of the blankets. They complained when their mother told them to herd the cows.

"I'll be glad when we get to Boonesborough," Betsey confided in a sly, proud voice. "Samuel Henderson, my future husband, is there, and he's got a slave or two, and when we get married, I won't have to do no heavy work ever again."

Martha snorted. "How do you know your husband won't make you toil as hard as any slave?"

Elizabeth jabbed her sister so she would be quiet. She looked curiously at Betsey. She seemed so young. How was it that she could soon be married? "When's your wedding day?" Elizabeth asked.

"Don't know just yet. Maybe next summer," Betsey replied importantly. She gave the cow a stinging flick of a willow branch. "Papa's deciding that. Betsey's getting married, too, but not till year after next, Papa said."

Elizabeth felt even more awkward and clumsy than ever walking beside the nearly grown-up and married Callaway girls.

"You got a sweetheart?" Fanny asked Elizabeth.

Elizabeth blushed and shook her head.

Betsey turned to Martha. "How about you?"

Martha frowned. "Don't have one and don't want one, neither."

The Callaway girls giggled, holding their hands to their mouths in a pretty, fetching fashion. "Elizabeth, do you know a sure way to find out who your true love will be?"

"Let me tell her," Betsey interrupted. "On the first day of May, hold a mirror over a well and look backward, and you'll see your future husband. Since it ain't the first of May and we don't have no well, there's another way you can tell. Just repeat after me:

"If I am to die a maid,
Let me hear my grave box made.
If I am to wed and sing,
Let me hear a little bird sing."

The four girls stopped walking and listened intently to the sounds in the woods. The trees shifted in the wind and shook down more leaves. Acorns fell making a *pock-pock-apock* sound. But they heard no bird call. Betsey and Fanny laughed. "Too bad," Betsey said.

"Don't seem too promising," Fanny added. "Guess you won't be wed and sing."

Elizabeth bit her lip. *An old maid!* She felt ashamed and unlucky.

"Pay no attention to those Tuckahoe girls," Martha whispered to Elizabeth. "What do they know? Come on. Let's walk ahead." She took Elizabeth's elbow.

"I can walk by myself." Elizabeth shook herself free. She walked a few steps behind her sister. Not once did she hear a bird call.

The rest of the morning a mizzling rain and glowering sky hid the mountains. Elizabeth kept to herself, humming a sad, solitary tune to Chinkapin and Blue:

"Go away, old man, and leave me alone,
For I am a stranger
And a long way from home."

The hatchet marks among the trees that marked the trace were confusing. Several times up Wallen Ridge they seemed to backtrack past places they had already climbed. Pa stopped and studied the pines. The trees were so dark and thick, it was impossible to see the sky or get their bearings from neighboring landmarks.

"We lost?" Mrs. Callaway demanded, tugging their horse along the trail.

"No," Pa replied, grinning as best he could, "we're just a bit bewildered, that's all."

Mrs. Callaway did not seem to think Pa was very funny. Finally, by following a steep, rocky slope, they managed to reach what seemed to be the top of Wallen Ridge. To the west in the distance they could at last spy Powell's Valley.

"What's that, Pa?" Elizabeth asked, pointing to a distant high, imposing white cliff.

"Part of the Cumberland Mountains. And below us there on the way to the Cumberlands is the valley Colonel Callaway spoke of." He announced that the company would stop to rest and hunt. While Pa and Austin primed their rifles to shoot squirrels or anything else they could find for supper, Elizabeth sat on a fallen log that overlooked the valley. She slipped out her book.

"Read!" begged Little.

"More!" demanded Big.

Martha stood with her hands on her hips. "We want to know what happens next."

Fanny and Betsey came closer, holding hands and asking sweetly, "Please?"

Elizabeth relented. She opened the book and began reading aloud about how Mr. Gulliver met the Imperial Majesty of the little people, who ordered an enormous wheeled wooden platform be built to carry Mr. Gulliver to a great building where he was to be kept prisoner. After days of being confined, he was allowed to stand up and realized what a tiny kingdom he now inhabited.

> ". . . I LOOKED ABOUT ME, and must confess I never beheld a more entertaining prospect. The country round appeared like a continued garden, and the enclosed fields, which were generally forty foot square, resembled so many beds of flowers. The fields were intermingled with woods . . . and the tallest trees, as I could judge, appeared to be seven foot high. . . ."

"I could climb that tree easy!" Big announced.

Elizabeth did not pay any attention to her brother's boast. She looked down into the valley and felt as if she understood how Mr. Gulliver might have felt from his great height. Everything below seemed as small as the kingdom of the little people.

"Hello! Hello!" a loud voice echoed.

"Papa!" Betsey and Fanny jumped to their feet. Elizabeth quickly shut the book as Colonel Callaway appeared from between the trees. His face was bright red and his horse was lathered and exhausted. Drake and Wright stumbled up the trail behind him.

"Did you find sign of him?" Mrs. Callaway demanded.

Colonel Callaway swung down out of his saddle. He took off his felt hat and wiped his sweaty forehead. He shook his head. "Went back nearly ten miles east. It was impossible to make certain which prints were his and which were ours. When we get to Martin's Station, I'll post a notice. I'll find him if it's the last thing I do. Unless of course the Cherokee already got him."

Elizabeth watched the colonel wipe down his horse with great care—the kind of gentle attention he never seemed to exhibit toward anyone in his family. "Excuse me, sir. But did you see any sign of our dog on your way?" she asked as bravely as she could.

"No, I did not," Colonel Callaway replied.

"Course a dog has no more sense than a slave. You can be sure both will turn up eventually." He laughed heartily.

What's so funny? Elizabeth turned away. She knew exactly where Enoch was headed. Home to his wife and child. For the first time, she hoped he would reach his destination safely.

The company walked twelve miles the next day through the wide rolling valley through the afternoon and into the evening. Finally, when everyone had just about given up hope, they came upon Martin's Station, a log structure with a stout gate made of logs. From the inside they could see a light burning. "Hello?" Colonel Callaway shouted in his booming voice. "Anyone home?"

"Who be there?" came a thin, raspy voice from the other side.

"Travelers from the Holston seeking shelter," Pa said. "Open the gate, Captain Joseph Martin."

The gate swung open and out stepped Captain Martin himself, a most remarkable-looking man. He was dressed as close to an Indian as anyone Elizabeth had ever seen, except for the fact that over his chest he wore a blue sash, now mostly faded and grimy. Pinned to one shoulder was what appeared to be a silver medal. His white hair matched his white beard. On his head he wore an amazingly bright red macaroni hat adorned with a long white plume. That his hat did not match his fringed calico shirt did not seem to bother him at all.

"Before you enter," Captain Martin said in a solemn voice, "you must swear allegiance to the king."

"What king?" Pa asked suspiciously.

"King George, of course. What other is there? As the Virginia Agent for Indian Affairs and the most influential person both with Indians and scattered settlers in this entire valley, I have many responsibilities. One of them is making sure all who pass are loyal to the Crown. Are you loyal to the Crown? Raise your right hand if you are."

"He's an old mad fool," Wright said under his breath.

"He is indeed," Austin whispered.

"Who are you, you most impertinent creature?" Captain Anderson demanded.

"No one special, sir," Wright replied quickly. "Only do you know we're at war?"

"With whom?"

"With King George himself," Wright said.

Captain Martin staggered backward. He leaned against one of the walls to catch his breath. "I can't believe that. I cannot. No one told me."

Captain Callaway gave Wright, Drake, and Austin threatening looks. "I'm sure it's just a small disagreement. Let us in to rest and add to our supplies. Our money's good."

"Of course, of course," Captain Martin said, waving the group inside. "You're welcome to buy what little I have. A pound of flour. Some salt. A bit of bacon. Are you sure about the war?"

Colonel Callaway shrugged. "Our news is as old as everyone else's. These troubles are far away. We're too busy fighting Indians to pay much attention to other men's arguments."

Somehow this information seemed to soothe Captain Martin. He gladly showed them where to set up outdoor cooking fires and unroll their bedding for the night. A group of bedraggled women huddled in the corner of one of the cabins where Elizabeth's family was to sleep. Two smoked pipes. They did not speak while Elizabeth and her mother began unpacking their bedding.

"Hold the baby so that I can begin cooking, will you, Elizabeth?" Ma said. She handed Elizabeth squalling Mary and went outside.

Elizabeth tried jiggling the baby, rocking the baby, but nothing seemed to work. She kept wailing.

One of the dark-haired strangers in the corner stepped forward. She reminded Elizabeth of the Cherokee woman they had met at Little Salt Lick. *But can I trust her?*

"Not be afraid," the woman said. She smiled, revealing a mouth with only two teeth visible. "I am wife of Martin. Called Grasshopper—seventh daughter of a full-blood Cherokee from Deer Clan. My father *Adawehis,* powerful conjurer. Your baby, what her name?"

"Mary," Elizabeth said slowly, holding her close. "She's all right."

"You lie," Grasshopper said in an even voice. "She very sick."

Mary wailed louder. Elizabeth took a deep breath. "She's got thrush."

"I am faith healer. I cure bleeding. I cure burns. I cure thrush. Let me see her?"

Elizabeth wasn't sure she should let the stranger take the baby. What would Ma say? She hesitated. They had tried everything. It was true. Mary was sick. Very sick. What harm could there be in letting this woman try?

"If no cure, these blisters can infect the baby's stomach and kill her," Grasshopper said slowly. "There's white thrash, yeller thrash, and black thrash. Yeller thrash hardest to cure. Comes up in clear blisters and poor baby can't eat. Can't drink. I cure all kinds. This baby's got yeller thrash. Mouth so sore she can't swallow. Let me have her."

Reluctantly Elizabeth handed the old woman the baby. Mary cried louder. Grasshopper spoke to Mary in some language Elizabeth did not recognize. She crooned and crooned, but Mary only cried louder. When the baby let out a particularly loud scream, Grasshopper cupped her fingers around Mary's mouth, and then she made a breathing motion as if she were sucking the breath away from the child. She did this three times, each time blowing the baby's breath over her shoulder.

"There," said Grasshopper, handing the baby back.

Elizabeth inspected Mary. She did not seem any better. In fact, she was crying harder than ever. Nervously she thanked the mysterious old woman and put Mary over her shoulder. "What should I give you for payment?" Elizabeth asked.

"What you have?" Grasshopper answered.

Elizabeth thought and thought. There had to be something. "I can tell you a story," she said, rocking Mary. "Have you heard of Mr. Gulliver?"

"A story? That is good." Grasshopper motioned to the two other women. They sat on the cabin floor and filled their pipes with fresh tobacco. "Tell about Mr. Gulliver."

Elizabeth sat on the unrolled bedding. She lay Mary on her folded knee and rubbed her stomach. She cleared her throat. She told everything she remembered from the book. How Gulliver was shipwrecked. What happened when he reached the land of the little people. How he went to another land where he was very small and everyone else was as large as giants. She told how he was captured by a farmer and how he had to defend himself against a bird that tried to swoop down and grab him. She told how he tripped over a snail shell and fell inside a molehill.

Each time she described an adventure, she had to stop while Grasshopper translated for the other women. "A foolish man," Grasshopper said. "Why he not travel with rifle?"

Elizabeth did not know. She had never considered this before.

"Tell more story."

Elizabeth told everything she knew. By the time Ma returned, Mary had fallen peacefully asleep.

"She seems better," Ma said, picking up the baby.

"Grasshopper did it," Elizabeth said, motioning to the faith healer.

Ma edged toward the door with the baby. "You coming to eat, Elizabeth?" she asked anxiously.

Elizabeth stood up. Before she left, she turned one last time and thanked Grasshopper for what she had done for Mary.

Grasshopper blew a cloud of smoke. "This Mr. Gulliver," she said and nodded, "he must need be careful."

Sept 20

We leav Martin Stashun early. Colnl leavs sign posted if anyone sees Enoch. Don't think nobody will. Maybe he got killd by Indiens. No sign of Just. Mary is better and the Blisters is mostly gone. Ma is glad; So am I We had this Creek to cross many times & very bad steep banks. Callaway saddle turned and the load all fell in. We got out. This Evening Austin kills two deer. Betsey bosses her Sister intolerable. Dont see how Fanny stands it. Course she is not alloud to have Opinens of her own

Sometimes as they walked along, Elizabeth felt as if she were traveling under a great body of water, bigger than any river, any lake. Branches—some leafy, some bare—crossed and crisscrossed high overhead. Even at midday the light seemed underwater green and dim yellow. Thick, spongy carpets of bright moss grew underfoot. Some places on the trail enormous curled roots stout as fences forced Big and Little to clamber over with difficulty.

It seemed to Elizabeth that the farther west they walked, the more the wilderness swallowed them whole. For weeks they'd seen no other buildings, no wood smoke curling from another settler's fire. In this vast forest the girth of some trees stretched wider than the biggest cabin back home. There were trees so tall, she couldn't see their tops. And everywhere on the forest floor lay the dead giants—twisted, shattered, fallen trees now cloaked in moss. Sometimes, while peering through the monstrous dark shapes, Elizabeth worried they'd never find their way out.

For two days the company had followed the trace that seemed to wind higher and higher up into the hills. Elizabeth could tell that the path was coming up to the top of a ridge when she could see the first glints of sunlight. And when she and her sister finally arrived in that place, they had to blink hard because the light hurt their eyes. They automatically held out their bare arms to feel the delicious warmth that never penetrated the darkness of the forest. Sometimes the brief blasts of sunlight made Elizabeth sleepy, and she longed to curl up in the pool of warmth and nap, but she couldn't. They had to keep moving—always westward.

They followed a trough-shaped valley between hills thickly covered with laurel and rhododendron. "Indians call this place Wah-see-o-to," Colonel Callaway said. "'The mountains where deer are plenty.'"

There was good hunting here, and no one went hungry, even though Elizabeth and her brothers and sister were tired of the taste of meat. Ma tried to soothe their complaints by calling roast turkey "bread" and bear "meat," but somehow that did nothing to make them happy. What they all wanted to eat was sweet tender new corn or better yet a hunk of wheat bread.

"Come on!" Martha called to Elizabeth, who lunged ahead in front of Big and Little. "Who'll make it over Cumberland Gap first?"

"Isn't fair for you to race ahead and not push

or pull one of these little ones," Elizabeth complained.

Martha slowed down and took Big's hand. He was too tired to complain or resist her help.

It took all of Elizabeth's energy to place one foot in front of the next. With every step she saw that the side of the mountain that the trail followed seemed to grow steeper and steeper until it stood straight up, leaving hardly more than a pass way for a grown person or a horse. On the other side of the trail the forest fell away. The last two or three hundred feet the mountain became a vertical cliff of white limestone. As she walked, she ran her hand along the rough edges as if by doing so she could prevent herself from tumbling over the edge.

"Wait for us!" Betsey whined. She and Fanny trudged along not speaking to each other. They kept their eyes on their feet and on the path ahead.

"You're as slow as Christmas coming!" Elizabeth called to them. But when Fanny and Betsey looked up at her she could see that they weren't smiling at her joke.

Finally the trace did not wind any higher, and Elizabeth knew that they had reached the top.

There was something thin and fine about the air. When she sniffed she smelled the scent of pine and fog and great distance. She pulled Little along to a rocky ridge and perched there and said nothing. On this clear afternoon she could see nearly fifty miles over a sea of blue-crested timbered ridges, jagged cliffs, and ravines. Westward stretched a lonely sea of treetops. No wisp of smoke from any settler's clearing. The only sign of another human habitation would be from Shawnee or Cherokee campfires.

The sight of so much more wilderness took her breath away. She could not speak. *Where is Caintuck? How far?* Somehow she had hoped that by reaching the Cumberland Gap, they'd be able to see their destination. Perhaps even spot the clearing and the rising smoke of Boonesborough. But, no, they still had miles and miles to go. Elizabeth slumped forward, leaning her elbows on her knees. Her brother did not say much. He curled against her for comfort, tucking his sore feet under himself.

"There it is!" Pa said expansively. He stood on another rock perch and gazed west, smiling.

What's he see that's so grand? "How long till we get there, Pa?" Elizabeth asked.

"Few more days maybe. Hard to tell." He took off his wide-brimmed hat and scratched his head. He licked his lips, not once taking his eyes from that distant horizon. "You can practically smell the game, can't you?"

Elizabeth did not reply. She watched Ma approach the same lookout with Mary in one arm. Her mother put her free hand to her eyes to shield them from the sun. When she looked out, her worried expression did not change.

Miles and miles yet. Elizabeth tried to imagine what Caintuck would look like, what it would smell like. But somehow she couldn't picture it. She'd have to see it first and decide then if it was like paradise or not.

Martha and Big seemed to drink in the far-reaching view of purple and blue-green mountains. "Moose and bears and otters and beavers!" Martha whispered. "Think of all those fine furs to trade."

"We'll be rich!" Big said in a hushed voice.

"First thing I'm going to do," Martha said solemnly, "is buy shoes."

Elizabeth couldn't help herself. She smiled. *That Martha!*

The trace took a northerly route as it scaled

down the other side of the gap. Colonel Callaway urged them on. "Better keep going," he said. "Warriors' Path follows this section, and it's not good to linger any more than we have to."

"What's Warriors' Path, Papa?" Betsey asked.

"The main route between Indian villages on Lake Erie and those to the south in Tennessee River country."

They took to the trail again, passing around the southern base of the mountain and emerging in the valley of Big Yellow Creek. On all sides were more mountains. Lengthening shadows filled the dark places between the trees, and soon it was time to rest and make camp for the night.

Elizabeth and her brothers and sister gathered firewood to begin a cooking fire. Drake, Wright, and Austin were busy unpacking the horses and setting them out on hobbles to graze.

"Indians!" someone shouted.

The men grabbed their guns.

Coming through the trees was a group of four Indians. *"Anoka!"* one of them cried. All four carried rifles. They were tall, and the hair on their heads was shaved except for a patch on the back of their heads where the hair hung long and was decorated with beads and feathers and stained deer skin. The oldest among them wore a breechcloth, a calico shirt, and a match coat over his shoulders. Like the others, he wasn't smiling.

Pa signaled to Colonel Callaway. Carefully Pa approached the oldest warrior, who appeared to be the leader. Pa made signs with his hands as he spoke.

"Can you hear anything?" Martha asked Elizabeth.

Elizabeth shook her head. She held each brother tightly by the hand. Ma's face was especially pensive and drawn. She kept Mary in her arms and stood close to the other children, watching every movement. They had no women, no children with them. Unlike the other Indians they had met, these men carried their rifles in the crooks of their left elbows at right angles across the front of their bodies. They did not put their guns down nor look away.

"Savages!" Mrs. Callaway said under her breath and spat.

"Will they kill us?" Fanny asked, her voice quavering.

"Quiet, girl," Mrs. Callaway replied.

After their talk seemed finished, Pa returned and told the rest what had been discussed. "They say we're in a neutral zone protected by their Great Father across the ocean," Pa said.

"*Who* in the blazes is that?" Drake demanded.

"King George," Pa replied. "They have many complaints against white settlers and hunters scaring off game. They say traders are cheating them. Soldiers burned their village, destroyed their crops, killed women and children, and sold others off as slaves."

No one spoke for several moments. "Will they let us pass?" Colonel Callaway whispered. He looked at the four men as if sizing up their strength.

"These Cherokee have been on a hunt for two days and have taken no animals. They lack powder," Pa continued.

"I sure don't want to give them none if I don't have to," the colonel murmured. "Next thing you know they'll be aiming their rifles at us."

"Might not have any choice," Pa said.

For once Drake was silent. Even Austin and Wright held their peace.

"Maybe they'll feel more friendly toward us on a full stomach," Pa said.

Ma did not say anything. Although it was clear she considered their dinner guests unwelcome, she chopped an extra big deer haunch, rubbed it with salt, and placed it in the pot over the fire.

"How many scalps you think he got?" Big whispered.

"Shut up," Elizabeth said. Once the food was ready, she watched the Indians hungrily eat trenchers of meat without speaking or looking at one another.

Martha watched the four visitors, too. She ate a few bites of meat, looking up often. Suddenly the oldest Indian glanced in her direction. He motioned for her to come closer. Gingerly Martha took a step forward at the same time Pa reached for his rifle. "Martha?" Pa said in a low, warning voice.

"It's all right, Pa," Martha replied.

The Indian reached up and took hold of one of her unruly black braids. He looked at it closely. Then he touched her arm, inspecting her skin. Carefully he held his own arm against hers. He looked closely into her dark eyes. With one hand he motioned for her to study the ground. He used his two fingers as if walking. Abruptly he took her arm and held it tight.

Martha appeared to be too frightened to scream.

Pa spoke to the Indian calmly. The Indian answered.

"What does he want?" Colonel Callaway demanded.

"He thinks she's a runaway from the village at Scioto," Pa said.

Quietly Drake, Austin, and Wright picked up their guns. The other three Indians did likewise. Elizabeth watched without being able to move or speak. She had a vision. Martha dragged away to some distant Indian village. *Gone forever.*

"Let me talk to him," Ma said in a bold, calm voice. She handed the baby to Elizabeth and came closer to the Indian who still gripped Martha by the arm. Ma sat on the ground and drew a circle in the dust. She motioned toward trembling Martha as if to indicate that this circle was Martha. She drew a line through the circle. She pointed to the empty half of the circle, then pointed to herself. In the other half she drew what appeared to be a broken arrow.

Suddenly the Indian smiled. He let go of Martha's arm.

Elizabeth took a deep breath.

The Indian removed his porcupine quill and glass bead necklace and put it around Martha's neck. He patted her on the head. He said something to the three men. They stood, ready to go. They took the bag of gunpowder Pa promised. As quickly as they had appeared, they disappeared.

Elizabeth felt her shoulders collapse. The tension in the air was gone. Even Drake seemed relieved.

"Guess we have a half Indian among us," Betsey announced.

Martha gave the eldest Callaway girl a nasty look.

"Better a half Indian than a dead Indian," Pa replied. He glanced anxiously at Ma. "Let's get dinner finished here."

But instead of handing out the remaining portions of meat from the kettle, she suddenly turned and left the campfire.

"What's wrong with her?" Colonel Callaway said, biting into his dinner with gusto.

Even from this distance Elizabeth knew. Ma was crying.

"She all right?" Elizabeth quietly asked Pa later, when no one else could hear. "We're safe now, aren't we? They aren't coming back."

Pa nodded. "They won't be coming back. But

only your ma can tell what's making her heart ache so."

This explanation only made Elizabeth more worried. What did he mean? She washed up the dishes and changed Mary's clothes. She made up a plate of food for Ma. But even after Ma crept back to camp, she said nothing, ate nothing.

That night wolves howled, and Pa kept the fire bright with new logs. Martha and the two boys and the baby slept soundly, wrapped in blankets. A new moon shone overhead. Elizabeth had trouble sleeping. She thought of the saying that Martha liked.

"New moon, true moon
Star in the stream
Pray tell my fortune
in my dream."

What if Ma's never happy again? She thought of her mother beside the fireplace back on the Holston. The little shoe. The way she cried. *Maybe I should tell Pa.* Then she recalled his words. "Only your ma can tell what's making her heart ache so." She'd have to ask Ma directly. It was the only way.

Someone stirred. "Ma?" Elizabeth called softly.

Her mother rose up on one elbow as if she'd been having trouble sleeping, too. "What's the matter? Are you sick? Let me look at you." Elizabeth struggled out of her blanket and sat close beside her mother with her feet to the fire. Ma brushed Elizabeth's hair back from her face. "You don't seem feverish," she said.

"I'm not sick," Elizabeth said. She glanced at her mother. "I just want to know if you're all right now."

"I'm fine." Ma looked away.

Elizabeth coughed nervously. "After the Indians left. It scared me. And I just wanted to know, just because . . ." She paused, unable to say anything more.

"You needn't worry. I'm not like Parthena's mother. I'll not wander off hearing voices and drown myself in the river."

Elizabeth took a deep breath. She did not want to speak of Mrs. Spikner and her many misfortunes. How after the last Indian attack she could not sleep and roamed about in the darkness, shuffling and looking under leaves and sleeping only during the day fully clothed with an ax under the bed. Ma was not like Mrs. Spikner, was she?

"I'm sad because of something that happened long, long ago, before you were born," Ma explained slowly. "I had a different husband then, before your father. His name was Wilson. I had a baby girl, too. Then one day in late October the settlement on the Clinch was attacked by a war party of Shawnee. My husband was killed. I hid and escaped. But the baby—" Ma paused and took a deep breath. "She was three years old. Same age as Little. She toddled out of hiding, and they found her and took her with them."

Elizabeth could feel her heart beating in her throat. She had never heard this story before. *They found her and they took her with them.* "Another sister?" she said in a kind of disbelief. At last she understood the little shoe. It had belonged to the other sister. The one who was taken away. "What happened to her?"

Ma shrugged. When she finally spoke again, her voice was filled with sadness. "She would be nearly fifteen by now."

An older sister. The one thing she had always wanted. "Where is she now?"

"I don't know. I never saw her again."

Elizabeth sat silent, stunned. It seemed as if the sister she had always wanted was given to her and taken away in the same breath. It seemed impossible. Incredible. *So many questions.* She did not even know where to begin. "What was her name? Did you try to find her?"

Ma sighed. "Her name was Amelia. And I thought I could not live without her. We searched and searched, but she had vanished without a trace. Maybe she's raised up by some other Indian family as one of their own."

One of their own.

"After it happened, some people in the settlement said my little girl would be better off dead than living with savages," Ma continued quietly. "But I never believed it. I wish her still to be alive. Maybe one day if I'm lucky we'll find each other again."

Elizabeth sat silent and hugged her knees to her chest. She could not keep her legs from shaking. *Somewhere I have an older sister. She doesn't know me. I don't know her.* The idea seemed fantastic, impossible—as crazy as the little people feeding Mr. Gulliver barrels of cider and whole sides of mutton as big as lark wings. *I wish her still to be alive.*

"You mustn't tell anyone," Ma said slowly.

"Not even Martha?"

"No. Not until she's old enough to understand."

Ma trusted her in a way she trusted none of the others. Elizabeth's new knowledge gave her a sense of importance, yet created a terrible burden at the same time. She stared into her lap and braided her fingers together. A half sister captured by Indians. Would she ever meet her? How would she know her? Betsey had said that captives sometimes never wanted to return to their original families. *She might never want to come home—*

"Now go to sleep," Mother said softly. "Tomorrow is going to be a long day."

Elizabeth did as she was told. But she could not sleep and stared up at the starry sky trying to imagine the eyes and voice of Amelia, the sister she had never met. That night she had a terrible dream. So terrible that she could not go back to sleep even though she tried over and over. Since there was no one to tell because everyone was asleep, she decided to write down what she remembered:

I dreamt we were back in the Holston. Some in our house were fighting for our lives, others wallowing in their blood, the House on fire over our heads, and the bloody Indians ready to knock us on the head if we stirred out. . . . No sooner were we escaped from the house but Pa being wounded in defending the house fell down dead, whearat the Indians scornfully shouted and hallowed and were presently upon him. Bullets flying thick, one went through my side and the same through the hand of my dear Child in my arms who I never saw before but I knew her. Big had his leg broke, which the Indians perceiving, they knockt him on the head. We was butchered standing amazed with blood running down to our heels.

When she was finished, the dream did not seem so frightening. Now she could see it laid out before her on the paper. She closed the book and finally went to sleep.

Chapter 11

Septembr 22

We is all overjoyd Just is back with us Even though he must ride acrost our packhorse because he can Hardly walk. Scratchd and limping but he found us. Wisht he could tell us Where he has been all this Time driving us crazy with worry. I notic Martha dont ware her indian Necklace no more. I dont ask but I suspect its in the Bottom of the cumberland River. Met a great maney people turnd back for fear of Indians but our Company goes on still with good courage. We come to a very ugley Creek with Steep Banks and Have to Cross several times on this creek. This is a very loury morning and like for Rain But we all agree to start early We crost Cumberland River and O, what a Long, solitary river it is! We travel down it about 10 miles through some Turrabel Canebrakes as we went down Callaways mair Ran into the river with her load and swam over He followed her & got on her & made her swim back again Then the rain came on powerfully until we were dripping We take up camp near Richland Creek Mrs. Calloway Bakes Bread without washing her hands we keep sentry this night for fear of Indians Told Martha this is the last of my ink

By midafternoon they stopped and set up camp. Two of the horses were lame, and Colonel Callaway decided to give them a rest. Big and Little snuggled up with Just and fed him choice bits of meat. The old dog had been tied to a tree so he wouldn't wander far. He seemed too tired to go anywhere. He lay on the ground with his lame leg to one side, tail thumping happily.

"You're spoiling that dog," Elizabeth said, smiling.

"No, we ain't," Big replied. "We're just glad to see him. He knows that."

Elizabeth found Pa cleaning his rifle. "What does it mean," Elizabeth asked, "when you dream of being shot?"

Pa stopped what he was doing and looked at

Elizabeth. "Such a dream," he said slowly, "means bad luck." Then he turned and spit over his left shoulder, the way he did whenever he needed to break a bad charm.

Elizabeth did the same. She hoped that by both of them spitting, they'd doubled the hex against misfortune. "What if I have the dream again?"

"Best way I know to avoid dreaming is to put both shoes under the foot of your bed at night. Never fails." Pa carefully examined the long slender rifle barrel.

"Will moccasins work?" she asked hopefully.

"No, you got to have real shoes with soles to keep nightmares away," Pa said. "Now, remember what I said. Don't wander out of camp tonight. Make sure your brothers and sister do the same."

"Yes, sir," Elizabeth replied absentmindedly. She didn't own any shoes. Neither did her brothers or sister. She'd seen Betsey's scuffed leather boots. She hardly ever wore them for fear of ruining them before her wedding day. Maybe she could convince Betsey to lend her the pair for one evening.

Elizabeth found Betsey and her sister wiping trenchers for their mother. They looked up when they saw Elizabeth walking toward them. "Your ears must be burning because we was just talking about you," Fanny announced. "Sit down."

Warily Elizabeth lowered herself onto a log. The Callaway girls smiled at her with so much friendliness, Elizabeth squirmed.

"We want to hear what happens to Mr. Gulliver," Betsey commanded.

Elizabeth glanced around the campsite. "Can't read unless Martha's here. I gave her my word I wouldn't finish the story without her."

Fanny yawned. "Who cares about Muddy Martha's feelings? We're bored."

"Read to us right now, and we'll be your best friends forever," Betsey said in a sweet, sly voice. "We promise."

Elizabeth thought about this offer. It was tempting. And yet she knew that if Martha saw her reading to the Callaway girls, she'd be hurt and angry.

"Hurry up and decide," Fanny said. "It's us or your stupid sister."

Elizabeth studied the Callaway sisters. There was something cold and cruel about their smiling mouths. Why hadn't she noticed before?

"Don't you want us to be your best friends?" Fanny demanded impatiently.

Elizabeth thought of Parthena. There was a best friend she could count on. Somebody who never let her down. Elizabeth could not say the same of Fanny and Betsey. Since the journey had begun, the only time they paid attention to her was when they were making jokes about her hair, her large size, her lack of sweethearts. They tolerated her presence only when she read to them.

"Sorry," Elizabeth said finally. "I'll tell you more about Mr. Gulliver when Martha comes—"

"We can't wait *that* long," Betsey interrupted.

Elizabeth felt confused. "What do you mean? Where is she?"

Betsey and Fanny exchanged guilty glances. "Last time we saw her was before supper," Betsey said. "She was running past those trees over there. Who knows when she'll be back?"

"Into the woods?" Elizabeth asked. Her stomach lurched. Why would Martha do anything so foolish? She knew Pa had forbade anyone to leave the campsite.

"Don't be letting on you're so upset," Betsey said. She elbowed her sister as if this were some great joke. "I should think that losing Muddy

Martha would be a great relief. I know I wouldn't want her for a sister."

Before Elizabeth could stop herself, she lunged forward, grabbed the front of the neck of Betsey's dress and yanked as hard as she could. The trembling older girl went flying toward her. "I wouldn't want *you* for a sister *or* a friend," Elizabeth hissed in Betsey's ear. She twisted the material harder. "Tell me again which way Martha went."

"That . . . that way," Betsey stammered. "She was carrying a basket."

Elizabeth released her grip. *Pokeberries!* She turned and ran to find her mother. There wasn't a moment to lose. In less than an hour it would be pitch black in the forest.

Ma's expression was stonelike when Elizabeth told her what had happened. "She should have been back by now. How will she find her way back in the dark?" Ma asked. Her voice became more agitated as she spoke. "We'll tell Pa. He'll know what to do." She thrust Mary into Elizabeth's arms. The damp baby began to cry.

Elizabeth felt awful. She watched helplessly as her mother half ran, half leaped across the campsite to Pa and told him the terrible news. Martha was missing.

Pa called together Drake and the other men. Colonel Callaway lit torches made from bundles of cane stalks. Each man carried a gun. The Callaway hound trailed on their heels. Just barked plaintively.

"Keep that dog tied so he don't chase after us. He won't make it far enough to be of any help, and I don't think none of us wants to be toting a dog through the woods," Pa said.

"Be careful!" Ma called.

Mrs. Callaway shook her head as she watched the men disappear between the trees. "Your daughter is causing us a peck of worry. You should have better trained her to stay close to home where's she's supposed to, not go roaming off foolishly in the dark where there's Indians and panthers and wolves."

Ma's eyes narrowed angrily. She scowled at Mrs. Callaway, then turned to the boys. "Come along, Big and Little. Time for you to get some rest."

Elizabeth sat beside Ma all evening, feeding the fire, while Mrs. Callaway and her daughters snored. Big, Little, and Mary slept peacefully.

Elizabeth's ears pricked forward at every sound. She waited anxiously to hear the colonel coming through the trees with Martha, chagrined and embarrassed but all in one piece. As she waited and waited, her hopeful vision began to fade.

Ma leaned forward, her eyes closed. Elizabeth nodded in the warmth of the fire. Suddenly she woke up. She could see the gray shimmers of dawn high above the trees. She felt stiff, after sleeping all night hunched forward leaning on her elbows. She looked around. Ma was gone and none of the men had returned. Elizabeth stood up quickly and searched the campsite. She saw Ma coming through the trees with a bucket of water. No one else was awake. No one stirred.

"She's not back?" Elizabeth whispered.

Ma shook her head. Her eyes were circled and tired, her face drawn. In that moment Elizabeth wanted to give her mother some kind of comfort. She wanted to say, "Don't worry. Martha can find her way around the forest."

But they both knew it was unlike Martha to disappear this long. *Something must have happened.*

Ma put another log on the fire and poked the smoldering embers. She put the kettle into the flames and began frying what was left of their meat. "Better milk the cow," she told Elizabeth. "Those men are going to be hungry after being out all night in the woods."

Elizabeth did not say anything. Her mouth was filled with a terrible sour taste. *It's my fault.* She tried to be even more helpful than usual just to prove to her mother that she really wasn't such an awful person. But somehow she could not convince herself.

All morning Big and Little played quietly by the fire. It almost seemed as if they knew something terrible had happened. Just howled. Big and Little jumped to their feet and ran toward Pa, who trudged into the campsite and wearily placed his gun beside a tree. Elizabeth watched nervously as he was followed by Colonel Callaway and the other men.

But no Martha.

"You didn't find her?" Mrs. Callaway asked.

Colonel Callaway shook his head. "We followed something like tracks for a while, but then when we reached the river, we couldn't follow them anymore. They'd vanished."

Pa slumped onto a log, his head in his hands. Elizabeth could only imagine what he was thinking. Martha, beloved Martha! *A true Poage.*

"There's no need to give up just yet," Ma said. Her voice sounded tight, anxious. "Martha's resourceful. She probably just fell asleep under a tree someplace. She knows what to do. She grew up in the woods."

Colonel Callaway sighed. "It's easy even for a grown man to get lost in there. One deer trail leads to another and pretty soon you're so turned around, you're spooked."

"A defenseless girl in the woods don't have much of a chance," Drake agreed.

No one spoke, but everyone was thinking about the same things. *Cherokee. Panthers. Wolves. Bobcat.* Ma cleared her throat. "Come eat something. We'll make a plan. You'll think better with a full stomach."

Wearily the men ate. Elizabeth poured each a dipperful of fresh water to mix with their whiskey. No matter how busy she kept herself stacking wood and busting up kindling with a hatchet, she still harbored lingering, worried images. Martha lost in the dark. Martha wandering in the woods. Martha meeting a panther—or a wolf or worse.

"Think she's ate up?" Big asked, tugging on Elizabeth's dress.

Elizabeth gave her brother a hard shove. "No, fool." But his words stung. They were truthful words she'd been thinking but felt too afraid to speak aloud.

For the first time she realized that her sister was more than just a bellyache. *She's somebody's precious.* Elizabeth couldn't imagine life without Martha. No more crazy ideas. No more pranks. No more fights. Parthena had said, "Nothing's ever dull around Martha." And she was right. Martha wasn't perfect, but she had spunk. She had imagination. *And she never let me down. Never.* Elizabeth sighed. *I want my sister back.*

That afternoon the search party went out again as soon as they'd finished eating. "We might not be back till nightfall," the colonel said.

"I don't know how long we can keep waiting here like this," Mrs. Callaway complained at sunset, when the men still had not returned. "It's dangerous leaving us here like this, women and children with no one to defend us. What if those four savages return?"

Fanny and Betsey refused to speak to Elizabeth. When they gazed at her, it was with cold, hateful stares. Most of the time they spent in whispering and watching the opening in the woods where they'd last seen their father disappear. *Maybe they're worried the forest will swallow him, too.*

When Pa and the others finally returned through the darkness, their silent voices and shuffling steps told the news. Martha was still lost. Colonel Callaway stayed in camp that evening with the other men, who fell into a deep sleep.

But Pa refused to give up looking. He went out for a second night carrying a torch made of cane, calling, calling. Just barked inconsolably. He wanted to go along, but Pa said no. "He's still too lame, too sick. He'll only be a burden."

That night no one spoke as they ate. The weather was getting colder, and they could see their breath. "Only got part of one deer haunch left," Mrs. Callaway said. "Somebody's got to hunt to keep the bodies going that's still living." She shot Ma a mean-spirited glance.

"Tomorrow we're going to have to move on. Snow's coming. We don't want to be on the trail when a blizzard hits," Colonel Callaway said. He did not look at Ma.

"If it were one of your daughters, would you

give up so easy?" Ma demanded. Her eyes were narrow and fierce.

Colonel Callaway still refused to meet her gaze. He still refused to reply.

Neither Ma nor Elizabeth slept that night. Every time Elizabeth shut her eyes, she had the same horrible dream again. The bad luck dream. She stayed awake, listening for a sign of Pa's rifle to signal that Martha'd been found. But there was no shot.

The next morning Just howled with happiness as Pa trudged into camp. Pa's eyes looked sorrowful as he slumped onto a log. "I looked everywhere, every creek, every hollow tree. I can't find nothing. No sign. It's as if she was swallowed up and disappeared straight into the earth."

Ma sat beside him and put a hand on his back—an unusual act of comforting in front of the others. "What are we going to do?" she murmured, patting his back the same way she did when she consoled fretting Mary. "What are we going to do?"

Elizabeth and her brothers watched their parents shyly, carefully, as if they were afraid they might see something they shouldn't. Meanwhile, the Callaways and the other men set about packing the horses. They were moving on. They were going to journey to Boonesborough before it snowed.

"We'll fresh notch the trees as we go," Colonel Callaway said, "so you can follow when you're ready." Wearily he began to put his goods in order. The camp seemed to move in slow motion. Nobody spoke much.

Elizabeth couldn't watch. She felt she had to do something. So much giving up and giving in all around her. It made her angry. She fed a piece of meat to Just, who ate heartily. *Well, I'm not waiting around to say goodbye.* She untied Just. She coiled his long rope around her arm and held him steady so that he wouldn't try to charge after the Callaway's hound again. "I'm taking Just," she said to no one in particular. Her parents seemed too stunned, too numb to notice.

Elizabeth headed into the woods. It felt good to walk, to get away from the sadness. She could not take very big strides because Just barely trundled along beside her as she walked. The dog limped but somehow kept going. His head down, he sniffed furiously. "You tired of being in one spot, too?" she demanded.

Together they followed the creek, all the time

keeping an ear for the campsite noise. Elizabeth did not want to get lost. The woods were dark and piney and silent. The sound that came from the campsite seemed to go no farther. The ground sprang beneath her feet as they rolled along, stepping over roots and patches of bright moss. "Slow down!" she called to Just, who tugged furiously and growled.

Elizabeth paused. *What's wrong?* She glanced over her shoulder. The hair on her arms rose up. Suddenly she wished she hadn't wandered away from the campsite. The trees loomed dark and menacing overhead. What kind of place was this that could swallow people and never leave a trace? First Amelia, then Enoch—and now Martha.

A branch creaked. *Whippoorwill! Whippoorwill!* A bird called. She took a hesitant step forward. Then another. "Martha?" she called softly. "Martha, where are you?"

Branches creaked overhead. Then, silence.

Just pulled and whimpered. "Hold on before you hurt yourself," she muttered. They walked across the creek. The water was clear and cold. Elizabeth stopped to scoop a handful and sip it.

While bent over, she felt something. Someone's eyes.

Slowly she stood up. What if somewhere, somehow, her other sister was watching? The half sister she had never met. Sleek and fast as a deer. If she lived here in this forest, she'd know every nook, every cranny. She'd know where Martha was, wouldn't she?

"Amelia?" Elizabeth called. But when she heard her own voice, she felt foolish, hopeless. *She's called something else now. A name I don't know.*

Elizabeth began to weep. She cried and cried—so hard and so long she frightened Just. He pulled on the rope as she sat on the stone, sobbing. Tick-plagued and mangy, Just put his ugly, scarred snout in Elizabeth's lap. He looked up at her with dark understanding eyes. "Precious old dear," she told him and blew her nose on her sleeve. "You're right. We might as well go back."

But when she took a few steps back the way they'd come, Just refused to follow. He kept pulling her, away from the creek, away from the path that led to their campsite. Elizabeth stumbled. She leaned over and untied the rope that was around Just's neck. At last she understood.

"Go!" she told him. "Go find her!"

The three-legged dog hobbled ahead, sniffing, sniffing. She wandered on and on after him, determined to keep up, even as she wondered how she'd get him home again if he collapsed. Could she carry him? How? The dog circled trees and snuffled under bushes. He kept moving and Elizabeth kept following. But he came up with no clues. No Martha.

Soon we'll be lost, too.

Elizabeth paused to wipe her forehead. She was sure by now Ma would be worried sick. *Three daughters lost.* But Elizabeth kept following Just. Finally, behind a rock outcropping, she heard something terrifying. "Stop!" she ordered Just. He stood still, his bent tail quivering.

In the distance, beyond the rocks, came eerie singing. A high clear distinctive voice emerged from nowhere and everywhere all at once.

"Blue Bird fly up
Give me my wish . . ."

Martha's haunt! Elizabeth gulped. She circled the place where the voice was loudest, strongest.

Still, there was no sign of Martha. *The song's her spirit.*

Just barked. He howled. He ran to a rock that was nearly covered in dead ferns and leaves. He made a terrible ruckus. Then he flopped down in exhaustion, panting furiously.

Elizabeth crawled closer. Something felt strange. A cool, misty breeze swept past her face, the way Parthena had always said a spirit entered a room. "Martha!" Elizabeth called. "Answer me!"

A ghostly, echoing voice shouted, "Elizabeth! Down here!"

"Where?" Elizabeth demanded. Frantically she pushed aside the brown, dry ferns. She saw an opening between the rocks.

"Down here!" Martha screamed. "I've fallen in a cave."

Elizabeth scrambled on all fours and pulled aside rocks. She could see into a hole, a dark black endless hole, but she could not spot her sister. "Are you all right?"

"My leg's not working so good. There's a bit of water down here. I'm so hungry I could eat a bull and it bellering," Martha said joyfully. "But other than that, I'm pretty good."

What should I do? Just looked too exhausted to lead the way back. She might never find this spot again if she were to go back for Pa and the others. She had to act. Now. *But how?* She looked down at the coiled rope at her feet. Quickly she tied a loop at one end. She lowered this into the hole. "Can you see the rope?"

"Barely."

"Can you reach it?"

"No. Can you send more?"

Elizabeth braced herself against a rock opposite the hole and lowered the hemp rope as far down as she could. She leaned over the hole with her arm extended, not even wondering what would happen if she fell in, too. "Grab it now!" She felt a slight tug. She smiled. It was Martha—not just a voice. Martha alive on the other end. "Can you slip the rope around your waist?"

"If I can just stand up, maybe."

The rope tugged and then was still again. "Martha?"

"Sorry. I just lost it. I'm trying again."

Elizabeth leaned as far in as she could. How far would she have to pull? *What if the rope breaks?* "Hold tight. Come on. Don't give up." She hoped her voice sounded bright and confident. She felt her sister tugging hard now. Elizabeth had to use all her strength and hold on to the rope with both hands. She pulled, hand over hand, bracing herself with one foot against the rock on the opposite side of the hole. Her back was damp with sweat. She pulled so hard she thought her shoulders would give out. But she did not give up. She kept pulling.

A hand. Martha's hand rose above the hole, searching for something, for a rock that would hold—anything. "Steady!" Elizabeth said between clenched teeth. "Don't want to drop you."

Little by little, Elizabeth inched Martha up out of the hole. Martha held tight to the rocks and managed to pull herself up out from the waist and roll away into the ferns with great difficulty. Her face was scratched and bleeding and her dress was torn. But she was laughing!

Elizabeth hugged her sister. *Nothing's ever dull around Martha.*

"I knew you'd find me," Martha said as Elizabeth collapsed beside her on the ground, exhausted and shaking. "You know how dark it was down there. No sounds except water. No light. Like the edge of the world. The first night

I kept quiet. I heard Indians camping nearby, and I didn't want them to find me."

"And the second night?"

"By the second night I started to feel afraid," Martha admitted. "So you know what I did?"

"What?" Elizabeth asked, smiling.

"I thought of Gulliver. I told the story over and over in my mind, and I imagined how he got through all those dangers and thought to myself how I could, too. I talked to those little people in Lilliput. I told them to go out and find you and bring you to me, and see, they did."

Elizabeth smiled and shook her head. *Where does she get such strange ideas?* "It was Just who found you. Come on, let's head back."

"I don't know if I can walk." Martha winced and struggled to stand.

"Put your arm around my neck, then. I'll help you," Elizabeth said. And together the two sisters followed limping Just back to the campsite.

September 27

Sad news this day Just dies;; old eager dog lay still in the morning before we had to leev and Big shouted Come on! But he wouldnt. We are all broke up over it. Buried him under a good heap of rocks. Big and Little could hardly keep from crying for they knew the dog long since they were borned. Martha too. He savd my life she says. It was a Hard time getting her to leev the bury spot we fixd so pretty with bunches of yellow witch hazel flowers. I miss that old stubborn howling when he heerd something at night. Pa said he was a Good Dog and will be sore missed. This morning the weather seems to be fair. When we meet another company turnd back Drake and Austin joins them like cowards. Good riddance. We go on & git to Loral river we come to a creek before wheare we are obliged to unload and toate our packs over on a log & swim our horses one hors Ran in with his pack and lost in the river & Pa got it again. Martha rides because her ankle still hurts.

September 28

This is a clear morning with Smart frost. We go on & have a very miry road. Martha rides. We campt this night on a creek branch of Lorel River and are surprised at campt By a wolf. Betsey and Fanny screem and scare it away. Big Grey creetur looked like Just except for his Yello eyes. Poor preshus old dear! I miss him yet. Read sum more about Guliver. herd of Buffaloe fantastik as Mr. Gulliver's Yahoo creatures. Very huge. Some walk, some run. At least 200. Others lope slow and careless with young Calves. Pa shoots one and we have a fine meal.

Sept. 29

Cloudy and warm we start early and go on about 2 miles down the River and then turn up a creek that we crost about 50 times some very bad Foards. Pa sees some very good land The Eavening we git over to the waters of Caintuck & go a littel down the creek & then we keep sentry the forepart of the night. It rains very hard. Martha walks some but mostly rides.

The next morning the air smelled of snow. Elizabeth and her brothers and sister wrapped blankets around themselves to keep away the cold as they ate their breakfast of jerked buffalo and cold water.

"When we get to the Caintuck settlement," Martha said, "there'll be bread. White and soft like cake. Much as you can eat."

"Who says?" Elizabeth asked.

"Pa." Martha licked her fingers. "They got corn and wheat and all good things at Boonesborough."

Big and Little chewed slowly. "When we're going to get there?" Big demanded as if he did not believe her. In all his life he had eaten white bread only three times.

"Today," Martha said. "I heard Colonel Callaway say we follow the Brushy Fork of Silver Creek till we see the Big Hill Range. Beyond is Caintuck River and Boonesborough."

Eagerly the boys helped Elizabeth and her sister pack up the horses. No one complained of the cold or the damp. They were almost there—almost to Caintuck!

"You little savages seem awfully bright and cheerful this morning," Betsey announced to Elizabeth and her sister. "We should be seeing our sweethearts soon, unless of course one of you wanders off again. There never was seen the like of you for mischief."

Martha scowled and clenched her fists.

"You has been a turrable wasting of our time," Fanny agreed.

Elizabeth held Martha's elbow to keep her sister's skinny knuckles from flying into Betsey's face. "No need to spat when we're this close," Elizabeth said in a slow, even voice. Betsey took a half step backward. "You don't want me to give you a black eye before you see your beau, do you, Betsey? He might think twice about marrying a girl who looks like a coon."

Betsey pursed her lips so that her mouth became a grim line. "Cohee!" she hissed and turned away. "Come along, Fanny."

"I could have beat her myself," Martha murmured as soon as the Callaway girls were gone.

"I know," Elizabeth replied. "Except sometimes a fistfight can cause more problems than it solves."

Martha looked at her in puzzlement. "Then why'd you tell her you'd punch her?"

Elizabeth smiled. "Just to scare her good. After all, I have to protect you. You're my little sister."

Martha made a face, but she seemed genuinely pleased with Elizabeth's answer.

All morning and into the afternoon they walked. The way was stony and slippery. At each turn, each opening between the trees, Elizabeth expected to see new sky, strange earth. A place like the one Pa had talked about—a garden where there was no forbidden fruit. A richer and more beautiful country than anything she had ever seen.

Finally, just as the sun began its journey down between distant hills, Elizabeth heard Pa whoop. She knew. *Caintuck!* Smoke curled overhead. She sniffed. Roasting corn! Her mouth watered and her stomach ached with a terrible longing. "Martha!" she shouted to her sister, who trudged behind her. "Come on, we're almost there."

Martha looked up at her with a bright, expectant expression. She waved the willow branch over the cow and hog. Blue and Chinkapin loped along, snuffling among the fallen acorns. The girls hurried together to the next opening between the trees. Below the ridge where they stood they could see the broad curve of the wide Kentucky River. Too excited to speak, they hurried faster.

"Don't it look like heaven itself, Ma?" Martha said.

Ma, who held Mary over one shoulder, seemed in no hurry to clamber down the next ridge. She shielded her eyes from the sun and gazed in the distance. "I count four, maybe six cabins there on the river. Not in a row but scattering. I thought Colonel Callaway said they was picketed and built up a real fort."

"Maybe they're working on it," Elizabeth replied. Eagerly she took Martha's hand and they hurried the rest of the way toward Boonesborough, which was located near the river. Opposite the fort were enormous sycamores rubbed white by large elk, deer, and buffalo who had come to sample the nearby sulphurous salt lick.

Just as Ma had said, there were no real stockade walls yet. No blockhouses. No fortified gate. Large gaps loomed between the half-dozen houses built haphazardly between stumps. Nearby stood a cleared field and what was left of a withering crop of corn, pumpkins, and cabbages. A welcoming volley of gunshots was fired into the air. Dogs bayed and barked. A pack of mutts gamboled toward them, circling, sniffing. Elizabeth waved them off with her switch.

A loud whoop echoed across the little valley. In a few moments a large group of people—mostly young men and slaves—came pouring out of the woods and fields and houses to take a look at the new arrivals.

"Hello, Captain!" Pa said and saluted a man only slightly taller than he was.

"Hello, Will," replied the soft-spoken captain. He was of average height, square built with broad shoulders, strong arms, and short legs. His forehead was large. He had a heavy brow, prominent cheekbones and a tight, wide mouth. Like many of the other men, he wore his dark hair plaited and clubbed in back, Indian fashion. He shook hands with Colonel Callaway, who for once seemed stumped for words.

"That's him," Martha whispered.

"Who?" Elizabeth said.

"Captain Boone."

Elizabeth was not impressed. She'd expected someone bigger, taller, younger. This ruddy-faced, pony-built man did not look one bit like the hero Pa had told stories about. Boone the best shot in Pennsylvania. The captain who licked the Shawnee on the Clinch. The leader who kept the settlers together at Castlewood when they all wanted to run. This quiet, undersize man looked ordinary.

Big and Little stood with their mouths open, gazing at the clutch of men who joked and hollered and whooped. They kept their eyes shyly on Captain Boone as if he were as wondrous and huge as a tremendous black bear that had suddenly wandered into the settlement. They seemed unable to speak or look away until Pa playfully rubbed the top of their red heads and gave them a shove toward their mother. "Go help your ma," he said.

Anyone could see that the boys would rather hang about the men and listen to their stories of midnight butcheries and captivities and horse stealings. The women were not included in this new leisure. Unlike the men, who could rest now that the journey had ended, Elizabeth's mother and the rest of the small group of women had to begin work in earnest.

"Somehow we're to make this place into a

home," Ma said and shook her head. Their unfinished cabin had no roof and no walls on two sides. "Looks like these fellows have been so busy dividing plots of land, they forgot about winter coming."

Elizabeth wondered how such a pitiful shack would keep out the wind and rain and snow. Mary, who sprawled on Ma's shoulder, let out a wail.

"She's a fair child," said a woman, who introduced herself as Rebecca Boone. She looked older than Ma—maybe thirty-five. Her back was stooped from so much time spent bent over a fire stirring a kettle or tending a haunch of meat. Gently she reached out to touch Mary's head. "Two months ago," she said in a low voice, "I buried my ninth baby. That was back on the Yadkin. Little boy. We called him William."

"Sorry to hear of your sorrows," Ma said.

Neither women spoke for a few moments.

"This your place?" Rebecca asked.

Ma nodded.

"Not much, is it?"

"Not yet."

Elizabeth scanned the crowd of men, who had become increasingly noisier now that a jug of whiskey was uncorked and passed around. She knew they'd have no more help from Pa that day.

"That pretty one your daughter?" Ma asked. She pointed to the thirteen-year-old girl who had a Callaway sister linked on either arm. The girls laughed and whispered. A passel of young men followed them at some distance like dragonflies dodging after a swarm of mosquitoes.

Elizabeth watched the Callaway girls twitter and tell secrets. For the first time, she did not feel jealous. Now she knew the truth. *They aren't really friends. They're only playacting.*

"Girls grow fast," Rebecca Boone said slowly. She turned and spoke to Ma in such a low voice, Elizabeth couldn't make out their murmurs. After a while the women parted.

Suddenly Little tugged hard on Elizabeth's skirt. "What do you want?" she demanded.

"We're going into the woods," Big replied, "to look for pokeberries. Martha's taking us."

Martha stood nearby, pretending to rub her toes clean with the hem of her dirty skirt.

"You don't need to do that, Martha," Elizabeth replied. "I can find my own."

"I want to," Martha said in a bashful voice. "I got another favor to ask."

"What?"

Martha took a deep breath. "Will you teach me to read?"

Elizabeth was so surprised, she couldn't think what to say. *Won't Mr. Feeny be pleased when I write and tell him?*

"Then I can read to you about Gulliver," Martha continued without looking at her sister. "Will you?" she added softly, as if this fragile plan were something she'd been hiding for a long time.

Elizabeth nodded and grinned. "If you go in the woods, don't go far."

Martha and the little boys dashed off between the trees.

"Elizabeth!" Ma called. "Where's your sister traipsing off? Doesn't she know we need her to help us begin housekeeping?"

"She'll be back soon," Elizabeth replied. "Let her go a while."

Ma looked curiously at Elizabeth as if she could not quite believe what she was hearing. Elizabeth did not pay any attention. She was too busy admiring the wail-away sweetness of Martha's voice, so tried and true, that echoed across the Caintuck trees and hills.

Thousands of settlers traveled west on the Wilderness Road after the Poages made their trip in 1775. As game rapidly disappeared and the Indian way of life was threatened, displaced Mingo, Shawnee, and Cherokee reacted with increasing hostility. Easy tribal access to British guns during the American Revolution intensified violence. Atrocities were committed by both Indians and whites. Kentucky became known as "a dark and bloody ground."

In February 1776 William Poage moved his family to Harrodsburg. According to an early Kentucky account, "In the spring of that year he cleared ground and planted corn two miles from the fort." In August 1777, Elizabeth's youngest sister, Ann, was born.

During the two years the family lived in Harrodsburg, Poage used his great mechanical skills to create all the wooden vessels used by the people in the fort. He was also responsible for the woodwork of the first plow and the first loom used in Kentucky. The spinning wheel carried by the Poages from the Holston was reportedly Kentucky's first as well. Described as a woman of "rare energy and ingenuity," Elizabeth's mother created some of Kentucky's earliest cloth using wild nettles and buffalo wool since the first flax crop wasn't ready.

On September 1, 1778, William Poage was killed in an ambush while traveling with sixteen men heading to another nearby station or fort. Elizabeth's mother remarried, this time to John Lindsey, who was killed at the Battle of Blue Licks in 1782. She remarried a fourth time. Her last husband was James McGinty.

Elizabeth seemed to have inherited her mother's energy and resiliency. She married John Thomas in 1785, when she was twenty-one years old. She had twelve children and lived to be eighty-six, which was considered very old at the time. She died in Harrodsburg on October 10, 1850. Much of what we know about her was recorded by Lyman C. Draper, a tireless collector of information about Daniel Boone. Draper traveled throughout Kentucky's back hills on his stout little pony named Nanny. He interviewed Elizabeth in 1844. "Near Harrodsburg," he wrote, "I found a Mrs. Thomas who was among the emigration to Kentucky in 1775; her memory is excellent; she was in Harrodsburg fort during the siege of 1777; from her I gathered many facts."

What happened to the Callaway sisters? On July 14, 1776, the girls joined Jemima Boone in a canoe ride on the Kentucky River. During their outing, they were kidnapped by a war party of two Cherokees and three Shawnees. Two days later they were successfully rescued by a group of settlers led by Boone. The next month Betsey, who was not quite sixteen, married Samuel Henderson—one of her rescuers. Boonesborough's first wedding was celebrated with watermelons, "the only delicacy." The next year Fanny and Jemima, who were both fourteen, were married as well.

Documents

Adair-Hemphill Papers, The Filson Club Historical Society, Louisville.

Draper Manuscripts, State Historical Society of Wisconsin, Madison. Including interviews by John D. Shane.

Durrett Collection, University of Chicago Library, "Mrs. Mary Dewee's Journal from Philadelphia to Kentucky, 1788."

Published Books

Arnow, Harriet S. *Seedtime on the Cumberland.* New York: Macmillan, 1960.

Arnow, Harriet S. *Flowering of the Cumberland.* New York: Macmillan, 1963.

Aron, Stephen. *How the West Was Lost: The Transformation of Kentucky from Daniel Boone to Henry Clay.* Baltimore: Johns Hopkins University Press, 1996.

Chester, Raymond Young, ed. *Westward into Kentucky: The Narrative of Daniel Trabue.* Lexington: University Press of Kentucky, 1981.

Corkran, David. *The Cherokee Frontier: Conflict and Survival, 1740–62.* Norman: University of Oklahoma Press, 1962.

Cushin, Joan E. *A Family Venture: Men and Women on the Southern Frontier.* New York: Oxford University Press, 1991.

Dicken-Garcia, Hazel. *To Western Woods: Breckinridge Family Moves to Kentucky, 1793.* Madison: Associated University Press, 1991.

Drake, Daniel. *Pioneer Life in Kentucky: 1785–1800.* New York: Henry Schuman, 1948.

Federal Writers' Project, American Guide Series. *Kentucky.* New York: Harcourt Brace and Co., 1939.

Jakle, John A. *Images of the Ohio Valley.* New York: Oxford University Press, 1977.

Kissell, Mary Lois. *Yarn and Cloth Making.* New York: Macmillan, 1918.

Lawlor, Laurie. *Daniel Boone.* Morton Grove: Albert Whitman, 1989.

Lester, William. *Transylvania Colony.* Spencer: Samual R. Guard and Co., 1935.

MacKay, Percy. *Tall Tales of the Kentucky Mountains.* New York: George H. Doran Company, 1926.

Perkins, Elizabeth Ann. *Border Life: Experience and Perceptions in Revolutionary Ohio Valley.* Evanston: Northwestern University Ph.D. Dissertation, History Department, 1992.

Pusey, William Allen. *The Wilderness Road to Kentucky.* New York: George H. Doran Co., 1921.

Ranck, George W. *Boonesborough.* Filson Club Publication Number 16. Louisville: Morton and Co., 1901.

Rohrbough, Malcolm J. *Trans-Appalachian Frontier, 1775–1850.* New York: Oxford University Press, 1978.

Speed, Thomas. *The Wilderness Road.* Louisville: The Filson Club, 1886.

Thomas, Lindsey and Thomas, Lucy B., *Kentucky Superstitions.* Princeton: Princeton University Press, 1920.

Tunis, Edwin. *Frontier Living.* New York: Thomas Y. Crowell, Co., 1961.

Williams, Clark. *The Redeemed Captive.* Amherst: University of Massachusetts Press, 1976.

Williams, Samuel C., *Early Travels in the Tennessee Country: 1540–1800.* Johnson City: Watauga Press, 1928.

Woodmason, Charles. *The Carolina Backcountry on the Eve of Revolution.* Chapel Hill: University of North Carolina Press, 1953.

Woodward, Grace. *The Cherokee.* Norman: University of Oklahoma Press, 1963.

About the Author

Trained as a journalist, Laurie Lawlor worked for many years as a freelance writer and editor before devoting herself full-time to the creation of children's books. She enjoys many speaking engagements at schools and libraries, and her books have been nominated for many awards. She lives in Evanston, Illinois, with her husband, son, daughter, and two large Labrador retrievers. Her books include the *Addie Across the Prairie* series, the *Heartland* series, *How to Survive Third Grade, The Worm Club, Gold in the Hills,* and *Little Women* (a movie novelization). Her nonfiction work, *Shadow Catcher: The Life and Work of Edward S. Curtis,* won the Carl Sandburg Award for nonfiction (1995) and the Golden Kite Honor Book Award (1995).

Turn the page for a preview of
the next American Sisters hardcover
Pacific Odyssey to California, 1905
by Laurie Lawlor

Available in July!

At the harbor in Honolulu the ship anchored and passengers began to climb down a long gangplank to awaiting smaller boats that would take them to shore. Impatiently, Su-Na and her sisters watched the line of Chinese, Japanese, and Korean travelers disembark. When it was their turn, Su-Na held tight to her sisters' hands. There were few children on board and she felt as if everyone was watching them. Anxiously, she followed Father, who helped Mother along as she walked with slow steps.

The other passengers, who were mostly men, politely made way for Mother. Like children, women were rare on the ship. In spite of several weeks of illness, Mother looked surprisingly beautiful. With skin like pale clouds and eyes the color of raven's wings, she moved as gracefully as bamboo bent by the wind. Once she self-consciously touched the back of her head. Su-Na knew that Mother was most proud of the beautiful black hair that reached nearly to the back of her knees. She wore it coiled up on her head the way a proper married woman should.

Su-Na watched her Mother walking ahead of her. Like her two sisters, Su-Na had what Mother called "boar's hair," thick and stiff hair that was almost impossible to manage. Su-Na knew that neither she nor her sisters shared their mother's beauty. And this fact, among many others, was clearly a disappointment to Mother. Like almost all Korean women, Mother's marriage had been arranged. She did not meet Father until their wedding day. "It is a pity you are not more attractive," Mother once told Su-Na. "Since we have so little money for your dowry, beauty might certainly help find you a good match."

Su-Na felt perfectly satisfied being exactly the way she was. She had no interest in being married and going off to live in a stranger's house to be a slave to a nasty mother-in-law. At this moment she was delighted to be in Hawaii, where she did not have to worry about ancient wedding customs.

Su-Na's family and the other Koreans inched into the building, which was filled with long tables and benches. Su-Na laughed when she saw her little sister weaving side to side as she walked. "There's no spring to solid ground," Jae-Mi declared. She kept expecting to have to lean at the next lurch of the ship. She felt oddly unpleasant.

Now that Su-Na was confined in the echoing building, she, too felt strange. The whole world was quiet. The other passengers from the S.S. *Iberia* filed silently into the room and took seats. Were they aware of the change as well?

"This is where we will eat our first meal," Father said, clearly impressed by the clean, spacious room. "In Hawaii we will be well taken care of." Father was a small, compact man with large, extravagant dreams. He talked constantly about all the things they would accomplish and with what pride his parents would greet them upon their successful return.

Father passed a nearly empty table and motioned for his family to sit at another spot already crowded with Koreans.

"Why not sit here, Father?" Su-Na asked. There were only three other men seated at this table. They did not wear trousers but instead had long robes with wide sleeves.

"Absolutely not. Please do not question my decisions," Father said angrily. He pointed to a bench. "Take a seat."

"Japanese," Mother murmured distastefully.

Father shook his head. "Dwarfish villains."

"What?" Jae-Mi asked and glanced curiously over her shoulder. Except for their clothing, the dwarfish villains looked no different from the hungry Koreans. This was a great disappointment. "Are Japanese the same as—"

"Silence!" Father barked. "Stop staring. Turn around." Jae-Mi did as she was told. Obediently, she and her sisters waited for their dinners. They were surprised to discover that there was no *kimchee,* no Korean rice, no vegetables cooked the way they liked. Instead the meal was simply rice and red fish. Su-Na and her sisters sniffed in fascination. They had never eaten red fish before.

Father signaled that they would begin with a prayer. That accomplished, Su-Na and her sisters began eating with gusto. Only their mother did not seem interested in the food. She picked at the fish with her chopsticks and kept glancing nervously around at their fellow travelers. At home the women never ate with the men. Yet here she was sharing a table with complete strangers—close enough to touch sleeves. Would she ever become accustomed to this new life?

"Eat," Father told Mother. "We do not know when we will have a hot meal again."

Mother made a face and put her chopsticks on the table, indicating that she was finished. "Look at this rice! Too dry. The cook must not know anything." She was very proud of the way she cooked rice, a skill she had learned from her mother so that when she moved in with her mother-in-law, she would not be criticized.

"Father, when can we go exploring?" Jae-Mi demanded. She thought the fish was delicious, salty and sweet at the same time. "When do we see our new house?"

"And our new clothes and shoes," Hi-Jong added eagerly.

"Enough!" Father said. "Eat when you eat. Talk when you finish." He scowled at his daughters. They had been in Hawaii only a few hours and already he felt as if he were losing control.

Meekly, the girls finished eating and placed the chopsticks on the table. Mother pouted and stared at her fine hands. They all jumped when a man with a loud voice shouted in a language they did not understand.

"What's he saying, Father?" Su-Na asked.

"He speaks Chinese," Father said. "He's calling names. I think he is taking roll to see if everyone is here and accounted for. Come, we will go closer so that I can hear him call our name."

Father stood up and gathered their belongings. The man with the loud voice divided the passengers into several groups to be sent to different plantations on different islands. Father and most of his friends from Seoul were sent to the Ewa Plantation on the island of Oahu. Each man lined up to have his name marked in a book and to receive a small metal disc with a number. They were warned to keep these discs safe.

"We will not go to a different island. We will take the train," Father said, beaming. He tucked the disc carefully in his pocket.

"The train?" Mother was shocked. This sounded dangerous. They had never been on a train before. "What if we are killed?"

"Don't worry. It's safe," Father replied. "We'll simply follow the crowd."

Su-Na and her sisters stayed close to Father as he made his way to the long steel path. They waited nervously until an enormous metal snake snorted and smoked directly toward them.

Mother clenched her eyes shut. Su-Na held tight to her sisters. Only Jae-Mi fearlessly studied the monstrous train. "Get on. Hurry," Father said, once the train stopped and the doors opened.

Mother seemed frozen, so Su-Na pushed her sisters forward. They climbed the steps into the train and discovered a long, narrow room with hard, wooden seats. It was crowded with other nervous passengers squeezed into the seats. Father almost had to carry Mother onto the train she was so terrified. "Sit," he said. Su-Na and her sisters lowered themselves into empty spaces. Mother did the same. As soon as Mother sat, she began to pray.

Without warning, a deafening bell rang. The narrow room lurched and rocked faster and faster. "Look!" Jae-Mi cried. She pointed at the windows where limbless trees flew past so quickly they seemed to lean halfway to the ground. Luxurious, green countryside rushed past. "Oh," Jae-Mi whispered, "isn't this like the Garden of Eden?"

Father smiled at her, but no one else paid any attention. Mother and Hi-Jong were too frightened to look out the window. Su-Na caught a glimpse of people. All kinds of people. None of them seemed to be Korean. This surprised Su-Na. Some wore broad hats; others had strangely pale faces. She spied people standing in green fields. They had dark skin and bright clothing. Some of the women wore large pieces of fabric wrapped around their heads. Some didn't. Some rode horses and waved at the train, their mouths open and their bright white teeth showing in the way that was forbidden among women at home. One of the women twirled around and around with a man.

Su-Na stared, even though she knew it was rude. *What strange manner of women are these?* She wondered how they had escaped from their homes and were allowed to travel alone in broad daylight. Proper

Korean women in veils could only go out after the curfew bell had sounded in town and all the men were off the streets. They were never allowed to be seen dancing with men in public.

"Look at her!" Jae-Mi said.

"Don't wave to those evil creatures," Mother warned. Her eyes were wide open and her expression was one of shock.

Green, lush hills sped past. "Hawaii is indeed even more beautiful than I had imagined," Father said.

The cattle were fat and plentiful in fenced-in places. The air that blew in through the open train window smelled of fragrant flowers. The houses they passed were small, only one or two stories high. They seemed to be built of wood and straw and were a dull cream color. Bright green grass carpeted the front of these houses, surrounded by bright flowers and blossoming shrubs. Su-Na wondered if they would live in such a beautiful house.

Much too quickly for Jae-Mi, the train ride ended. Jae-Mi and Hi-Jong clutched their father's hands as they stepped off the train onto the wooden platform. Here another man with a loud voice bellowed for them to climb onto another train car. This car had no walls, no windows and no proper seats. It was just a flat shelf with wheels. Father said it was used to haul sugarcane from the fields to the mill. None of the girls knew what this meant. They took a seat in the middle of the car. Mother followed them awkwardly.

Jae-Mi decided it would be exciting to sit in the open and speed along. She was disappointed to discover that this train crawled slowly along the track.

"What's this?" Su-Na asked. She picked up a green stalk mostly stripped of broad leaves. There were many such stalks scattered on the train car. At one end the stalk oozed something white and sticky. When Su-Na licked her fingers, the sap tasted sweet.

"Sugarcane," Father said. He smiled and pointed to the great green stalks rising up on all sides of the track. Row upon row of tall cane whispered in the wind. In the distance, great smokestacks reached nearly to the sky, higher than any building back home. There was a sweet, burning smell in the air.

The black smoke curling up from the smokestacks reminded Hi-Jong of the guardian dragon painted on the temple door back home. "Are there dragons here?" she asked hopefully.

"No," Father said, and laughed. "That is the sugar mill."

"Oh," Hi-Jong replied. So far Hawaii had been a big disappointment. No bright clothing, no new shoes, no sweet rice cakes, and no dragons. She had not spied one hat sprouting from the ground or one bolt of silk dangling from a tree. Once again she wondered if the grown-ups had deceived her.

"We're almost there. Our new house looks very fine, doesn't it?" Father said with great enthusiasm. He pointed in the distance to a row of whitewashed cabins that reflected the late afternoon sun.

The girls nodded. Mother shrugged and sighed. Finally the train car stopped. The man with the loud voice gave directions. The Korean workers filed off to their camp in the east. The Chinese marched to the north and the Japanese hurried to the west. In the center was the mill and another group of buildings.

"There are more Japanese and Chinese than Koreans," Su-Na said to Father.

Father nodded and made a clicking noise with his tongue as if he thought this were a great pity.

Su-Na cleared her throat. "Everywhere we go we travel together, and yet we never speak. Why is that, Father?"

Father grunted and picked up their roll of bedding.

"Is it because we do not understand each other's language?" Su-Na asked, remembering the Chinese man in the dining hall who called out names. "If we knew each other's language do you think—"

"Silence!" Father said impatiently. "Must you ask so many questions? It is unseemly for a girl. Now help your mother."

Su-Na frowned as soon as Father turned away from her. She grabbed Jae-Mi and Hi-Jong by the hand and hauled them off the train. In paradise there was supposed to be no confusion, no unhappiness. *Why do I feel so mixed up?*

Out of nowhere a man galloped up to them on a fine white horse. He waved his brown, American-style hat and smiled at them. He spoke Korean and told them that his name was Boss Jung. "This way, my fellow countrymen," he announced. Father and the other new Korean workers looked relieved. "I have been in Hawaii three years. I am the all-around man here. Interpreter, camp boss, preacher, mail carrier, and language teacher."

The crowd laughed. Boss Jung held up a small metal disc with a number stamped on it. "Do not lose your *bango,*" he said. "This is how you will be paid every month. No *bango,* no pay. From now on, this will be your new name. You work hard, *hana-hana,* and you do all right."

Father stared at the *bango* in his hand. Slowly, he repeated aloud: "46571." This was Father's new name.

"Hana-hana," Su-Na whispered. She stared out at the cane fields and could see the men and some women moving along the rows. Some were hoeing, others were chopping down the ripe cane. "There are women, Father. Do they have *bangos* too?"

Father rubbed his chin thoughtfully. "I suppose. And I suppose they are paid, as well."

"Perhaps I should work in the fields. We will need the money," Mother said in a quiet voice.

Father's face darkened. "Even if we have to starve, I will not have you working in the fields."

Mother meekly followed Father to the row of cabins that would be their new home. Unlike the Uncles and Second Uncles, who shared a long barracks-style house, the few married men with families had their own small houses. Su-Na's family's house had a thatched roof made of grass.

They slipped off their shoes the same way they did at home and stepped high over the doorstep to make sure that no unfortunate luck followed them inside. The floor was hard-packed dirt. Inside the one small room there was no furniture, only a shallow fire pit. A scorpion with many legs hurried across the floor.

Mother gasped and scurried out again. Father had to hunt in all the dark corners and up and down every wall to prove to her that there were no more ferocious beasts waiting to ambush her. "See?" he said, smiling. "All gone." He handed a broom made of twigs to Su-Na. Su-Na and her sisters swept the place clean and unrolled the bedding. The family was so exhausted, they did not bother to eat anything for dinner and quickly fell asleep.

* * *

It came as a great shock the next morning when the plantation siren blasted at five o'clock. *Br-r-row-aw-ie-ur-ur-rup!*

Shrill voices echoed through the camp. Someone shouted in English and banged on the cabin door. *"Hana-hana, hana-hana,* work, work." Suddenly the door swung open. A huge, white-skinned *luna* burst in, screaming and cursing. The foreman grabbed the blankets off Father. Mother screamed. Su-Na hid under her blanket with her sisters. *"Hana-hana, hana-hana,"* the *luna* shouted and left.

Father quickly pulled on his work clothes and hurried outside. Su-Na crept to the doorway and watched as up and down the row of cabins the laborers appeared from the shadows like ghosts. They coughed and lit cigarettes. Few spoke. Some carried hoes. She strained her eyes to see her father, but he was soon swallowed up in the gangs of workers. It was clear that no one would be allowed to lie under a palm or a bread tree and do nothing.

Even food was not free. As soon as Su-Na and her sisters finished helping Mother roll up the bedding and carry water from the pump, they had to accompany her to the plantation store. Mother needed a bag of rice and a small crock of *kimchee.* "What number?" the store clerk demanded. He only knew a few words of Korean.

"Number?" Mother asked shyly.

"*Bango* number," Su-Na whispered. "It's 46571," she told the clerk. Carefully, she studied the way he wrote down the number and the cost of their food.

"How do we know he doesn't cheat us?" Mother hissed as they turned to leave with the supplies.

Su-Na pushed open the door. "We don't," she said. "Even though we are only staying here a short while, perhaps we should learn to speak English."

Mother frowned. "Your father would not like that. But then, of course, he must realize that we have to survive as best we can." She gave Su-Na a sly look. "I know you will learn quickly."

"Me?" Su-Na asked. This burden seemed unfair. "What about Jae-Mi and Hi-Jong?"

"They will learn, too. As soon as I can, I am enrolling all three of you in school. Now come along, little pigeons," Mother said.